"What the hell is the matter?"

Jamie couldn't meet Ryan's eyes, but she had to when she felt his fingers on her chin and she was roughly made to look at him.

"You're my boss! I work for you!"

"I want more than your diligence. I want you in my bed, where I can touch you wherever I want. I'm betting that that's what you want, too—whether you think it's right or wrong. In fact, I'm betting that if I touch you right now, right...*here*—" Ryan trailed his finger along her cleavage and watched as she fought to catch her breath "—you're not going to be able to tell me that you don't want me, too...."

"I don't want you..."

"Liar!" He kissed her again, and her lies were revealed in the way she clutched at him, not wanting to, but utterly unable to resist.

CATHY WILLIAMS was born in the West Indies and has been writing Harlequin® romance novels for some fifteen years. She is a great believer in the power of perseverance as she had never written anything before (apart from school essays a lifetime ago!), and from the starting point of zero has now fulfilled her ambition to pursue this most enjoyable of careers. She would encourage any would-be writer to have faith and go for it! She lives in the beautiful Warwickshire countryside with her husband and three children, Charlotte, Olivia and Emma. When not writing, she is hard-pressed to find a moment's free time in between the millions of household chores, not to mention being a one-woman taxi service for her daughters' never-ending social lives. She derives inspiration from the hot, lazy, tropical island of Trinidad (where she was born), from the peaceful countryside of middle England and, of course, from her many friends, who are a rich source of plots and are particularly garrulous when it comes to describing her heroes. It would seem from their complaints, that tall, dark and charismatic men are way too few and far between! Her hope is to continue writing romance fiction and providing those eternal tales of love for which, she feels, we all strive.

Books by Cathy Williams

Harlequin Presents® Extra

109—HIRED FOR THE BOSS'S BEDROOM
141—A SPANISH BIRTHRIGHT
169—IN WANT OF A WIFE?

Other titles by this author available in eBook

HIS CHRISTMAS ACQUISITION
CATHY WILLIAMS
~ One Christmas Night In... ~

TORONTO NEW YORK LONDON
AMSTERDAM PARIS SYDNEY HAMBURG
STOCKHOLM ATHENS TOKYO MILAN MADRID
PRAGUE WARSAW BUDAPEST AUCKLAND

Recycling programs
for this product may
not exist in your area.

ISBN-13: 978-0-373-52841-7

HIS CHRISTMAS ACQUISITION

First North American Publication 2011

www.Harlequin.com

Printed in U.S.A.

HIS CHRISTMAS
ACQUISITION

CHAPTER ONE

JAMIE was late. For the first time since she had started working for Ryan Sheppard she was running late due to an unfortunate series of events which had culminated in her waiting for her tube to arrive, along with six-thousand other short-tempered, frustrated, disgruntled commuters, so it seemed.

Wrapped up against the icy blast that raced along the platform—whipping her neatly combed hair into frantic disarray and reminding her that her smart grey suit and smart black pumps might work in an office, but were useless when faced with the grim reality of a soggy London winter— Jamie pointlessly looked at her watch every ten seconds.

Ryan Sheppard *hated* late. In fairness, he had been spoiled with her because for the past eighteen months she had been scrupulously early—which didn't mean that he would be sweetly forgiving.

By the time the tube train roared into view, Jamie had pretty much given up on getting into the office any time before nine-thirty. Because nothing would be gained from calling him, she had resolutely refused to even glance at the mobile phone hunkered down in the bowels of her bag.

Instead, she reluctantly focused her mind on the main reason why she had ended up leaving her house an hour later than she normally would have, and sure enough, all thoughts of her sister successfully obliterated everything else from her mind. She could feel the thin, poisonous thread of tension begin to creep through her body and, by the time she finally made it to the spectacular, cutting-edge glass building that housed RS Enterprises, her head was beginning to throb.

RS Enterprises was the headquarters of the massive conglomerate owned and run by her boss, and within its stately walls resided the beating pulse of all those various tentacles that made up the various arms of his many business concerns. An army of highly trained, highly motivated and highly paid employees kept everything afloat although, at quarter to ten in the morning, there were only a few to be glimpsed. The rest would be at their desks, doing whatever it took to make sure that the great wheels of his industry were running smoothly.

At quarter to ten in the morning, *she* would normally have been at her desk, doing her own bit.

But instead…

Jamie counted to ten in a feeble attempt to dislodge her sister's face from her head and took the lift up to the director's floor.

There was no need to gauge his mood when she pushed open the door to her office. On an average day, he would either be out of the office, having emailed her to fill her in on what she could be getting on with in his absence, or else he would be at his desk, mentally a thousand miles away as he plowed through his workload.

Today he was lounging back in his chair, arms folded behind his head, feet indolently propped on his desk.

Even after eighteen months, Jamie still had trouble reconciling the power house that was Ryan Sheppard with the unbearably sexy and disconcertingly unconventional guy who was such a far cry from anyone's idea of a business tycoon. Was it because the building blocks of his business were rooted in computer software, where brains and creativity were everything, and a uniform of suits and highly polished leather shoes were irrelevant? Or was it because Ryan Sheppard was just one of those men who was so comfortable in his own skin that he really didn't care what he wore or, for that matter, what the rest of the world thought of him?

At any rate, sightings of him in a suit were rare, and only occurred when he happened to be meeting financiers—although it had to be said that his legendary reputation preceded him. Very early on Jamie had come to the conclusion that he could show up at a meeting in nothing but a pair of swimming trunks and he would still have the rest of the world bowing and scraping and asking for his opinion.

Jamie waited patiently while he made a production out of looking at his watch and frowning before transferring his sharp, penetrating black gaze to her now composed face.

'You're late.'

'I know. I'm really sorry.'

'You're never late.'

'Yes, well, blame the erratic public-transport system in London, sir.'

'You know I hate you addressing me as *sir*. When I'm knighted, we can have a rethink on that one, but in the meantime the name is Ryan. And I would be more than happy to blame the erratic public-transport system, but you're not the only one who uses it, and no one else seems to be running behind schedule.'

Jamie hovered. She had taken time to dodge into the luxurious marble cloakroom at the end of the floor so she knew that she no longer resembled the hassled, anxious figure that had emerged twenty minutes earlier from the Underground station. But inside she could feel her nerves fraying, unravelling and scattering like useless detritus being blown around on a strong wind.

'Perhaps we could just get on with work and…and…I'll make up for lost time. I don't mind working through lunch.'

'So, if it wasn't the erratic public-transport system, then what kept you?' For the past year and a half, Ryan had tried to get behind that calm, impenetrable facade, to find the human being behind the highly efficient secretary. But Jamie Powell, aged twenty-eight, of the neat brown bob and the cool brown eyes, remained an enigma. He swung his feet off his desk and sat forward to stare at her with lively curiosity. 'Hard weekend? Late night? Hangover?'

'Of course I don't have a hangover!'

'No? Because there's absolutely nothing wrong with a little bit of over-indulgence now and again, you know. In fact, I happen to be of the opinion that a little over indulgence is very good for the soul.'

'I don't get drunk.' Jamie decided to put an immediate stop to any such notion. Gossip travelled at a rate of knots in RS Enterprises and there was no way that Jamie was going to let anyone think that she spent her weekends watching life whizz past from the bottom of a glass. In fact, there was no way that she was going to let anyone think anything at all about her. Experience had taught her well: join in with your colleagues, let your hair down now and again, build up a cosy relationship with your boss—and hey presto! You suddenly find yourself going down all sorts of unexpected and uncomfortable roads. She had been there and she wasn't about to pay a repeat visit.

'How virtuous of you!' Ryan congratulated her with the sort of false sincerity that made her teeth snap together in frustration. 'So we can eliminate the demon drink! Maybe your alarm failed to go off? Or maybe…'

He shot her a smile that reminded her just why the man

was such a killer when it came to the opposite sex. For anyone not on their guard, it was the sort of smile that could
bring a person out in goose bumps. She had seen it happen
any number of times, watching from the sidelines. 'Maybe,'
he drawled, eyebrows raised speculatively, 'there was someone in your bed who made getting up on a cold December
morning just a little bit too much of a challenge…?'

'I would rather not discuss my private life with you, sir—
sorry, *Ryan.*'

'And that's perfectly acceptable, just so long as it doesn't
intrude on your working life, but strolling into the office at
ten in the morning demands a little explanation. And fob-
bing me off with promises to work through your lunch isn't
good enough. I'm an exceptionally reasonable man,' Ryan
went on, tapping his pen thoughtfully on his desk and running his eyes over her tight, closed face. 'Whenever you've
had an emergency, I've been more than happy to let you take
time off. Remember the plumber incident?'

'That was once!'

'And what about last Christmas? Didn't I generously give
you half a day off so that you could do your Christmas shopping?'

'You gave *everyone* half a day off.'

'Point proven! I'm a reasonable man. So I think I deserve
a reasonable explanation for your lateness.'

Jamie took a deep breath and braced herself to reveal
something of her private life. Even this small and insignif-
icant confidence, something that could hardly be classed
as a confidence at all, went against the grain. Like a time
bomb nestling in the centre of her well-founded good in-
tentions, she could hear it ticking, threatening to send her
whole carefully orchestrated reserve into chaos. She would
not let that happen. She would throw him a titbit of infor-

mation because, if she didn't, then the wretched man would just keep at it like a bull terrier worrying a bone.

He was like that—determined to the point of insanity. She figured it was how he had managed to take his father's tiny, failing computer business and build it up into a multinational conglomerate. He just never gave up and he never let go. His sexy, laid-back exterior concealed a strong and powerful business instinct that laid down rules and watched while the rest of the world fell into line.

She opened her mouth to give him an edited version of events, filtered through her strict mental-censoring process, when the door to his office burst open. Or rather it was flung open with the sort of drama that made both their heads spin round simultaneously in surprise to the leggy, blonde-haired, blue-eyed woman who literally flew into the office. Her big, long hair trailed wildly behind her, a thick, red cashmere coat hooked over her shoulder.

She threw the coat over the nearest chair. It was a gesture that was so wildly theatrical that Jamie had to stare down at her feet to stop herself from laughing out loud.

Ryan Sheppard had no qualms about bringing his women into the workplace once he had signed off work for the day. Jamie had always assumed that this was the arrogance of a man who only had to incline his head slightly to have any woman he wanted putting herself out to accommodate him. Why go to the bother of traipsing over to a woman's house at nine in the evening when *she* could traipse to his offices and save him the hassle of the trip? When things had been particularly hectic, and his employees had been up and running on pure adrenalin into the late hours of the night, she had witnessed first-hand his deeply romantic gesture of sending his staff home so that he could treat his date to a Chinese takeaway in his office.

Not once had she ever heard any of these women complain. They smiled, they simpered, they followed him with adoring eyes and then, when he became bored with them, they were tactfully and expensively shuffled off to pastures new.

And such was the enduring charm of the guy that he still managed to keep in friendly touch with the majority of his exes.

But there had never been anything like this, at least that she could remember in her brief spell of working for him.

She couldn't help her snort of laughter at the unexpected sight of some poetic justice being dished out. She quickly tried to bury it under the guise of coughing, although when she caught his eye it was to find him glaring at her before transferring his attention back to the enraged beauty standing in front of his desk.

'Leanne…'

'Don't you *dare* "Leanne" *me*! I can't *believe* you would just break up with me over the *phone*!'

'Flying over to Tokyo to deliver the news face to face wasn't an option.' He glanced at Jamie, who immediately began standing up, because witnessing the other woman's anger and distress was something she would rather have avoided. But Ryan nodded at her to sit back down.

'You could have *waited* until I got back!'

Ryan sighed and rubbed his eyes before standing up and strolling round to perch on his desk. 'You need to calm down,' he said in a voice that was perfectly modulated and yet carried an icy threat. Leanne, picking it up, gulped in a few deep breaths.

'Cast your mind back the last two times we've met,' he continued with ferocious calm. 'And you might remember that I *have* warned you that our relationship had reached the end of its course.'

'You didn't mean that!' She tossed her head and her mane of blonde hair rippled down her back.

'I'm not in the habit of saying things I don't mean. You chose to ignore what I said and so you gave me no option but to spell it out word for word.'

'But I thought that we were *going* somewhere. I had plans! And what—' Leanne glared at Jamie, who was focusing on her black pumps '—is *she* doing here? I want to have this out with you in *private*! Not with your boring little secretary hanging on to our every word and taking notes so that she can report back to everyone in this building.'

Little? Yes. Five-foot-four could hardly be deemed tall by anyone's standards. But *boring*? It was an adjective that would have stung had it come from anyone other than Leanne. Like all the women Jamie had seen flit in and out of Ryan's life, Leanne was the sort of supermodel beauty who had a healthy disrespect for any woman who wasn't on the same eye-catching plane as she was.

Jamie looked at the towering blonde and met her bright-blue eyes with cool disdain.

'Jamie is here,' Ryan said in a hard voice, 'because, in case you hadn't noticed, this is my office and we're in the middle of working. I'm sure I made it perfectly clear to you that I don't tolerate my work life being disrupted. Ever. By anyone.'

'Yes, but…'

He walked across to where she had earlier flung the red coat and held it out. 'You're upset, and for that I apologise. But now I suggest that you exit both my offices and our relationship with pride and dignity. You're a beautiful woman. You'll have no trouble replacing me.'

Jamie watched, fascinated in spite of herself, by the transparency of Leanne's emotions. Pride and anger waged war with self-pity and a temptation to plead. But in the end she

allowed herself to be helped into her coat; the click of the
door as she left the room was, at least, a lot more controlled
than when she had entered.

Jamie studiously stared in front of her and waited for
Ryan to break the silence.

'Did you know that she was coming?' he asked abruptly
and Jamie turned to him in surprise. 'Is that why you chose
today, of all days, to get here two hours late?'

'Of course not! I wouldn't dream of getting involved in
your private life.' Although she had in the past: trinkets
bought for women; flowers chosen, ordered and sent; the-
atre tickets booked. On one memorable occasion he had actually taken her to a luxury sports-car garage and asked her
to choose which colour Porsche he should buy for a certain
woman who had lasted no longer than a handful of weeks.
He was nothing if not an absurdly generous lover, even if
his definition of a relationship never contained the notion of
permanence. 'And I don't appreciate being accused of...of...
ever being in cahoots with any of your bimb—girlfriends.'

Ryan's eyes narrowed on her flushed face. 'The reason I
asked was because you seemed to derive a certain amount
of satisfaction from Leanne and her display of histrionics.
In fact, I could swear that I heard you laugh at one point.'

Jamie looked at him. He was once more perched on his
desk, his long, jean-clad legs extended and lightly crossed
at the ankles. In heels, Leanne would have been at least six
foot tall and he had still towered over her.

Jamie felt a quiver of apprehension race down her spine
but for once she was sorely tempted to say what was on her
mind.

'I'm sorry. It was an inappropriate reaction.' Except she
could feel a fit of the giggles threatening to overwhelm her
again and she had to look down hurriedly at her tightly
clasped fingers.

When she next looked up it was to find that he was standing over her and, before she could push back her chair, he was leaning down, his muscular hands on either side of her, his face so close to hers that she could see the wildly extravagant length of his eyelashes and the hint of tawny gold in his dark eyes. He was so close, in fact, that by simply raising her hand a couple of inches she would have been able to stroke the side of his face, touch the faint growth of stubble, feel its spikiness against her fingers.

Assaulted by this sudden wave of crazy speculation, Jamie fought down the sickening twist in her stomach and carried on looking at him squarely in the face although she could feel her heart beating inside her like a jack hammer.

'What *I'd* like to know,' he said softly, 'is what the hell you found so funny. What I'd really like is for you to share the joke with me.'

'Sometimes I laugh in tense situations. I'm sorry.'

'Pull the other one, Jamie. You've been in tense situations with me before when I'm trying to get a major deal closed. You've never burst out laughing.'

'That's different.'

'Explain.'

'Why? Why does it matter what I think?'

'Because I like to know a bit of what's going on in my personal assistant's head. Call me crazy, but I think it makes the working relationship go a lot smoother.' In truth, Ryan didn't think that it would be possible to find anyone with whom he could have worked more comfortably. Jamie seemed to possess an uncanny ability to predict his moves and her calm was a pleasing counterpoint to his volatility.

Before he had hired her, he had suffered three years of terrific-looking fairly incompetent secretaries who had all developed the annoying habit of becoming infatuated with him. His faithful middle-aged secretary who had served him well for nearly ten years had emigrated to Australia and he had followed her up with a series of ill-suited replacements.

Jamie Powell really worked for him and it had nothing to do with the mechanisms of her mind or what she thought about him. But suddenly the urge to shake her out of her cool detachment was overwhelming. It was as though that shadow of a snicker that had crossed her face earlier on had unleashed a curiosity in him, and it took him by surprise.

He pushed himself away from her and walked across to the low sofa that doubled as a bed for those times when he worked so late that sleeping in his office was the easiest option.

Reluctantly, Jamie swivelled her chair in his direction and wondered how many billionaire bosses would be sprawled indolently on a sofa in their office in a pair of jeans and a faded jumper, hands clasped behind their heads, work put on temporary hold while they asked questions that were really none of their business.

Again that finger of apprehension sent another shiver down her spine. After a succession of unsatisfactory but emotionally important temp jobs, would she have taken this one if she had known the nature of the beast?

'I'm not paid to have thoughts about your private life,' she ventured primly in a last-ditch attempt to change the subject.

'Don't worry about that. I give you full permission to say what was on your mind.'

Jamie licked her lips nervously. This was the first time he had ever pinned her down like this, the first time he hadn't backed off when his curiosity had failed to find fertile ground. Now, like a lazy predator, he was watching her, gauging her reaction, forming conclusions.

'Okay.' She looked at him evenly. 'I'm surprised that this is the first time one of your girlfriends has seen fit to storm into your office and give you a piece of her mind. I thought it was funny, so I laughed. But quietly. And I wouldn't have laughed if I had left your office when I had wanted to, but you gestured to me to stay put. So I did. So you can't blame me for reacting.'

Ryan sat up and looked at her intently. 'See? Now isn't it liberating to speak your mind?'

'I know you think it's funny to confuse me.'

'Am I confusing you?'

Jamie went bright red and tightened her lips. 'You don't seem to have any morals or ethics at all when it comes to women!' she snapped. 'I've worked with you for well over a year and you must have had a dozen women in that time. More! You play with people's feelings and it doesn't seem to bother you at all!'

'So there's a lurking tiger behind that placid face of yours,' he murmured.

'Don't be ridiculous. You asked me for my opinion, that's all.'

'You think I use women? Treat them badly?'

'I...' She opened her mouth to tell him that she had never thought anything whatsoever about the way he treated women, not until this very moment, but she would have been lying. She realised with some dismay that she had done plenty of thinking about Ryan Sheppard and his out-of-hours relationships. 'I'm sure you treat them really well, but most women want more than just expensive gifts and fun and frolics for a few weeks.'

'What makes you say that? Have you been chatting to any of my girlfriends? Or is that what *you* would want?'

'I haven't been chatting to your girlfriends, and we're not talking about me,' Jamie told him sharply.

Her colour was up and for the first time he noticed the sultry depths of her eyes and the fullness of her mouth. She was either blissfully unaware of her looks or else had made a concerted effort to sublimate them, at least during working hours. Then he wondered how he had never really *noticed* these little details about her before. It occurred to him that they had rarely, if ever, had the sort of lengthy conversation that required eye-to-eye contact. She had managed to avoid the very thing every single woman he met sought to instigate.

'I treat the women I date incredibly well and, more importantly, I never give them any illusions about their place in my life. They know from the start that I'm not into building a relationship or working towards a "happy family" scenario.'

'Why?'

'Come again?'

'Why,' Jamie repeated in a giddy rush, 'are you not into building relationships or doing the happy-family thing?'

Ryan looked at her incredulously. Yes, he always encouraged an outspoken approach, both within the working environment and outside it. He prided himself on always being able to take what was said to him. He might choose to totally ignore it, of course, and did a great majority of the time, but never let it be said that he wasn't open to alternative opinions.

Except who had ever asked him such an outlandishly personal question before?

'Not everyone is.' But he was keen to bring the conversation to an end now. 'And, now that the cabaret show's over, I think it's time we get back to work.'

Jamie gave a little shrug and instantly resumed her professionalism. 'Okay. I didn't manage to find the time to look at those reports about the software company you're thinking of investing in. Shall I go and do that now? I can have everything ready for you by this afternoon.'

So, to Ryan's vague dissatisfaction, the day kicked off the way it always did: with Jamie working wonders with her time, sitting outside his office in her own private cubicle, where she did what she was highly paid to do with such staggering efficiency that he wondered how he had ever managed without her around.

His phone rang constantly; she fielded calls. The creative bods who worked on some of the games software three floors down burst into his office with some new idea or other, became over-exuberant; she ushered them out like a head teacher whose job it was to keep order in the classroom. When he made the comparison, his keen eyes noted the way she blushed and smiled, and then he grinned when she told him that she wouldn't have to play head teacher if he was a bit better at playing it himself.

At three, he grabbed his coat; he was running late for a meeting with three investment bankers. She told him at the very least to take off the rugby shirt and handed him something a little more presentable from the concealed, fully stocked wardrobe in the suite opposite his office. Everything was back to normal and it was beginning to grate on him.

At five-thirty, he got back to his office after a successful meeting to find her gathering her things together and slipping on her coat. About to switch off her computer, Jamie felt her heart flutter uncomfortably. She hadn't been expecting him to be back before she left.

'You're leaving?' Ryan tossed his coat over his desk and began pulling off the unutterably dull grey woollen jumper which he had obligingly worn for the benefit of the bankers.

Underneath, the white tee-shirt barely concealed the hard muscularity of his body. Jamie averted her eyes, mentally slapping herself because she should be used to all this by now and she wasn't sure why she was suddenly reacting to him like a complete idiot. Maybe it had something to do with her sister being back on the scene. There would be a psychological connection there somewhere if she could be bothered to work it out.

'I…I *would* have stayed on, Ryan, but something's come up, so I have to dash.'

'Something's *come up*? What?' He headed straight to where she was still dithering in front of her computer terminal and lounged against the door frame.

'Nothing,' Jamie muttered.

'Nothing? Something? Which is it, Jamie?'

'Oh, just leave me alone!' she blurted out, and to her horror she could feel her eyes welling up at the sudden intrusion of stress that had presented itself in her previously uncomplicated life. She looked away abruptly and began fiddling with the paperwork on her desk, before turning all her attention to her computer in the desperate hope that the man still leaning against the door frame would take the hint and disappear. He didn't. Worse, he walked slowly towards her and she felt his finger on her chin, tilting her face up to his.

'What the hell is going on here?'

'Nothing's going on. I'm just…just a bit tired, that's all. Maybe I'm…coming down with something.' She shrugged his hand off but she could still feel it burning her skin as she quickly stuck on her thick black coat and braced herself for the biting cold outside.

'Is it to do with work?'

'I beg your pardon?'

'Has something happened here at work that you're not telling me about? Some of the guys can be a bit rowdy. Has someone said something to you? Made some kind of inappropriate remark?' He suddenly blanched at the possibility that one of them might have seriously overstepped the mark and done something a little more physical when it came to being inappropriate.

Jamie looked at him blankly and shook her head. 'Of course not. No, work's fine. You'll be relieved to hear that.'

'Some guy giving you grief?' He tried to sound sympathetic but his imagination had broken its leash and was filling his head with all sorts of images that were definitely in the 'inappropriate' category.

'What kind of grief?'

'Has someone made an unwanted pass at you?' Ryan said bluntly. 'You can tell me and I'll make damn sure that it never happens again.'

'Why do you think that I would need help in sorting out something like that?' she asked coolly. 'Do you think that I'm such a fool that I wouldn't know how to take care of myself if some guy decided to make a pass at me?'

'Did I say that?'

'You implied it.'

'Other women,' Ryan said, his big body tensing, 'are probably just a bit more experienced when it comes to men. You... I may be mistaken, but you strike me as an innocent.'

Jamie stared at him. She distantly wondered how they had reached this point in the conversation. How many wrong turnings did it take to get from discussing a software report to her sex life—or lack of it?

'I think it's time I head home now. I'll make sure that I'm in on time tomorrow.' She began moving towards the door. She was only aware of him shifting his stance when she felt the hot weight of his fingers curled around her wrist.

'You were upset. Can you blame me for wanting to know why?' He gave a little jerk and pulled her towards him.

'Yes, I can!' Her mouth was dry and she knew that she was flushed. In truth, she felt as though her body was on fire.

'I'm your boss. You work for me, and as such you're my responsibility.' His eyes drifted down to her full mouth and then lower, to the starched white shirt, the neat, tailored jacket. He was aware of her breasts heaving.

'I am my own responsibility,' Jamie said through tight lips. 'I'm sorry I brought my stress to work. It won't happen again and, for your information, it has nothing to do with anything or anyone in this office. No one's been saying anything to me and no one's made a pass at me. I haven't had to defend myself but I'm just going to say this for the record— if someone *had* done something that I found offensive, then I would be more than capable of looking out for myself. I don't need you to step in and defend me.'

'Most women appreciate a man jumping to their defence,' Ryan murmured and just like that the atmosphere changed between them. He slackened his grip on her wrist but, instead of pulling away her hand, Jamie found herself staring up at him, losing herself in the depths of his eyes, mesmerised. She blinked and thankfully was brought back down to planet Earth.

'I am *not* most women,' she breathed. 'And I'd really appreciate it if you could let me go.'

He did, stepping aside, watching as she stuck on her coat and wrapped the black scarf around her neck.

She couldn't look at him. She just couldn't. She didn't understand what had happened back there but she was shaking inside. Not even the thought of Jessica could distract her from the moment. And she was horribly aware that he was staring at her, thinking that she was over-reacting, behaving like a mad woman when all he had done was to try and understand why she had been acting out of character.

She worked for him, and as her boss he had seen it as his civic duty to protect her from possible discomfort in her working environment, and what had she done in response? Acted like an outraged spinster in the company of a lech. She was mortified.

And then she had *stared* at him. Had he noticed? He noticed everything when it came to women and the last thing she needed was for him to think that she saw him as anything other than her boss, a man whom she respected but would always keep at arm's length.

'I've left those reports you asked me to do on your desk in descending order of priority,' she said crisply. 'Your meeting at ten tomorrow's been cancelled. I've rearranged it and you should have the new date updated onto your phone. So...'

'So, you can run along and nurse your stress in private,' Ryan drawled.

'I will.'

But she spent the entire journey back to her house dwelling on the tone of his voice as he had said that. She wondered what he was thinking of her. She didn't want to, but she did.

The barrier she had imposed that clearly defined both their roles felt as though it was crumbling around her like a flimsy pack of cards, and all because he had happened to catch her in a vulnerable moment.

Thanks to Jessica.

It was pitch-black and bitterly cold as she walked from the Underground station to her house. London was in a grip of the worst winter weather for twelve years. Predictions were for a white Christmas, although it had yet to snow.

In her house, however, the lights were on. All of them. Jamie sighed and reflected that, on the bright side, at least Jessica had managed to locate the key in its secret hiding spot under the flower pot at the side of the house. At least she had made it down to London from Edinburgh safe and sound, even if she brought with her the promise of yet more stress.

CHAPTER TWO

'But you don't *understand*...'

Jamie took time out from loading the dishwasher to glance round at her sister, who was wandering in a sulky fashion around the kitchen, occasionally stopping to pick something up and inspect it with a mixture of boredom and disdain. Nothing in the house was to her taste; she had made that very clear within the first few minutes of Jamie pushing open the front door and walking in.

The place, she'd announced, was poky. 'Couldn't you have found something a little more comfortable? I mean, I know Mum didn't leave us with much, but honestly, Jamie!' The furnishings were drab. There was no healthy stuff in the fridge to eat and, 'What on earth do you do for alcohol in this place? Don't tell me that you while away your evenings with a cup of cocoa and a good book for company?'

Jamie was accustomed to the casual insults, although it had been so long since she had actually set eyes on her sister that she had forgotten just how grating they could be after a while.

Their father had died when Jamie was six and Jessica still a three-year-old toddler and they had been raised by their mother. Jamie had been a bookworm at school, always studying, always mentally moving forward, planning to go to university. She left Jessica to be the one who curled her hair and painted her fingernails and, even at the age of thirteen, develop the kind of wiles that would stand her in very good stead with the opposite sex.

Jamie had never made it to university. At barely nineteen she had found herself first caring for her mother—who, after a routine operation, had contracted MRSA and failed to recover—then, when Gloria had died, taking on the responsibility of looking after her sixteen-year-old sister. Without Jamie even noticing, Jessica had moved from a precocious pre-teen to a nightmare of a teenager. Where Jamie had inherited her father's dark looks and chosen to retreat into the world of literature and books, Jessica had been blessed with their mother's striking blonde looks. Far from retreating anywhere, she had shown a gritty determination to flaunt as much of herself as was humanly possible.

A still-grieving Jamie had suddenly been catapulted into the role of caretaker to a teenager who was almost completely out of control.

What else could she have done? Gloria had begged her to make sure to keep an eye on Jessica, to look after her, 'Because you *know* what she can be like—she needs a firm hand…'

Jamie often wondered how it was that she hadn't turned prematurely grey from the stress of it.

And now, after all that muddy water under the bridge, stuff she still could hardly bear to think about, here was Jessica, back on the scene again, as stunning as ever—more, if that was possible—and already making Jamie grit her teeth in pointless frustration.

'I understand that you have responsibilities, Jess, and they may be getting to you but you can't run away from them.' Jamie slammed shut the dishwasher door with undue force and wiped her hands on a tea towel.

Dinner had been a bowl of home-cooked pasta with

chicken and mushrooms. Jessica had made a face and flatly refused to eat any of the pasta because she was off carbs.

'It's all right for you!' Jessica snapped, scooping up her poker-straight blonde hair into a ponytail before releasing it so that it fell in a heavy, silky curtain halfway down her back. '*You* don't have to deal with a bloody husband who works all the hours God made and expects me to be sitting around with a smile pinned to my face, waiting for him to return for a nice hot meal and a back massage! Like some kind of creepy Stepford wife.'

'You *could* get a job.'

'I *got* a job. I got eight jobs! It's not my fault if none of them suited me. Besides, what's the point me going out to work for a pittance when Greg earns so much?'

Jamie didn't say anything. She didn't want to think about Greg. Thinking about Greg had always been a downhill road. Once upon a time he had been her boss. Once upon a time she had fancied herself in love with him—a secret, pleasurable yearning that had filled her days with sunlight and made the burden of looking out for her younger sister more bearable. Once upon a time she had actually been stupid enough to think that he would wake up one day and realise that he cared for her in the same way she cared for him. Unfortunately, he had met Jessica and it had been love at first sight.

'Have you thought about volunteer work?' she offered, fed up.

'Oh, purr…leese! Can you *really* see me doing anything like that, Jamie? Working in a soup kitchen in Edinburgh? Or arranging flowers in the local parish church and doing fund raisers with the old biddies?'

She had dragged one of the chairs over and was sitting with her long legs propped up on the chair in front of her so that she could inspect her toenails which were painted a vibrant shade of pink.

'I'm bored,' she said flatly. 'I'm bored and I'm fed up and I want a life. I'm too young to be buried in the outskirts of Edinburgh where it rains all the time, *when* it's not snowing, hanging around for Greg, who only cares about sick animals anyway. Did you know he's got a fan club? The dishiest vet in town—it's pathetic!'

Jamie turned away and briefly squeezed her eyes tightly shut. It had been years since she had last seen Greg but she remembered him as clearly as if it had been yesterday. His kind face, the way his grey eyes crinkled when he smiled, his floppy blond hair through which he constantly ran his fingers.

The thought of her sister being bored with him filled her with terror. In the end, Greg had been her salvation. He had taken over the business of worrying about Jessica. Jessica might not need him, but she, Jamie, most definitely did!

'He's crazy about you, Jess.'

'Loads of guys could be crazy about me.'

Jamie felt her body go cold. 'What does that mean? Have you? You're not doing anything stupid, are you?'

'Oh, don't be such a prude.' But she sighed and leaned back against the chair, letting her head flop over the back so that she was staring glassy-eyed up at the ceiling. 'No, I'm not doing anything *stupid*, if by that you're asking me whether I'm having an affair. But the way I feel…'

She allowed that possibility to take shape between them and it was all Jamie could do not to slap her sister. However, years of ingrained caretaking papered over the passing temptation. This, she felt, was a subject best left alone in the hope that it might just go away. She was busy wondering what topic she could choose that might be safer when the doorbell rang.

'Someone flogging something,' she muttered, relieved for the distraction. 'Please, Jess, just give Greg a call. He must be worried sick about you.'

She left the kitchen to a disgruntled Jessica informing her that she had no intention of doing any such thing, that he knew perfectly well where she was, just like he knew that she needed some space.

Jamie wondered how long Greg would carry on waiting while Jessica hunted around for this so-called space she was intent on finding, and she was still chewing it over in her head as she pulled open the front door.

The sight of Ryan standing on her doorstep was so shocking that for a few seconds her mind went completely blank.

He had never, ever been to her house before. Not even when they had happened to drive out of London to attend a meeting. He had never picked her up or dropped her off. She hadn't even thought that he knew where she lived.

Eventually, her brain caught up with what her eyes were telling her, and she stopped gaping at him open-mouthed and actually croaked, 'What are you doing here?'

'You were stressed out. I was worried about you. I thought I'd drop by, make sure you were all right.'

'Well, I'm fine, so I'll see you tomorrow at work.' Belatedly, she remembered her sister scowling in the kitchen and she stepped outside and pulled the door quietly closed behind her, taking care not to shut it completely.

'How did you find out where I live?' she hissed under her breath. Under the lamplight, his face was a contour of harsh shadows and his eyes glittered in the semi-darkness. He was still in his work clothes, the jeans, the faded sweater, the trainers and the coat, which she knew had cost the earth, but which he wore as casually as if he had got it from the local Oxfam shop.

'Personnel files. It really wasn't too difficult.'

'Well, you have to go.'

'You're shaking like a leaf. It's cold out here—let me in for a few minutes.'

'No!' She saw his eyebrows rise fractionally and added, stammering, 'I mean, it's late.'

'It's eight-forty-five.'

'I'm busy.'

'You're on edge. Why? Tell me what's going on.' Ryan laughed. 'You're my indispensable secretary. I can't have you storing up nasty secrets and then suddenly deciding to walk out on me, can I? What would I do without you?'

'I...I'm obliged to give a month's notice,' Jamie stammered. Ryan Sheppard on her doorstep suddenly seemed to throw that all-important distance between them into confusion and she didn't like it.

'So you *are* thinking of leaving me. Well, it's a damn good thing I turned up here to get the full story out of you, isn't it? At least this way I can defend my corner.' For some reason he felt disproportionately let down by the thought of her just dumping a letter of resignation on his desk without any forewarning and then jumping ship. 'So, why don't you invite me inside and we can discuss this like two adults? If it's more money you're after, then name the amount and it's yours.'

'This is crazy!'

'I know. And I hate dealing with crazy.' He reached out and pushed the door open just as Jessica's petulant voice wafted from the direction of the kitchen, carolling to ask where Jamie was, because she really needed something to eat—and was there anywhere they could go for a halfway decent salad? She didn't fancy being cooped up for the rest of the night.

And then there she was, long and beautiful and blonde, and all the things that Ryan looked for in a woman, standing by the banister as Jamie turned around with a sigh of resignation. Stunningly pretty, stunningly fair-haired and dangerously bored with her husband.

If Jamie could have reached out and pushed Ryan straight back out of the front door, then she would have done so, but he was already inside the tiny hall, removing his thick coat while his eyes never strayed from Jessica.

'Well, well, well,' he drawled in a lazy undertone. 'What have we here…?'

'My sister,' Jamie muttered.

The glitter in Jessica's eyes mirrored his lazy speculation and Jamie felt a chill run down her spine.

There was no need for her to make introductions. Not when her sister was sashaying forward, hand outstretched, introducing herself—with, Jamie noted, her left hand stuck firmly behind her back.

'You never told me that you had a sister,' Ryan said, turning his fabulous eyes to Jamie.

Standing to one side like an uninvited spectator in her own house, Jamie's voice was stiff when she answered, 'I didn't see the relevance. Jessica doesn't live in London.'

'Although, I might just be thinking of changing that.'

Jamie's head whipped round and she stared, horrified at her sister. 'You can't!'

'Why not? I told you. I'm bored in Scotland. And, from what I see here, London certainly has a hell of a lot more to offer. Why did you never mention that you had such a dishy boss, Jamie? Did you think that I might dash down here and try to steal him from you?'

Jamie held on to the banister, feeling faint, and Ryan, lounging only feet away from her, took the opportunity to gauge the electric atmosphere between the sisters. Arriving unannounced on his secretary's doorstep had been a spontaneous decision which he had begun to regret on the drive over, but now he was pleased that he had made the journey.

'How long are you in London?' He looked at Jessica but his mind was still on Jamie and on that ferocious wall of privacy she had erected around herself. Purpose, he thought, unknown.

'She's literally only here for a day or two before she returns to Scotland. She's married and her husband will be waiting for her.'

'Did you have to bring that up?'

'It's the truth, Jess. Greg's a good guy. He doesn't deserve this.' *And* you *certainly don't deserve* him, she thought.

'I'm having lots of marital problems,' Jessica insisted to Ryan. 'I *thought* that I could come down here and find some support from my sister, but it looks like I was wrong.'

'That's not fair, Jess! And, besides, I'm sure Mr Sheppard doesn't want to stand here and listen to our family history.'

'Please, feel free to go on. I'm all ears!'

'You need to go.' Jamie turned to him. Every muscle in her body felt like it had been stretched to snapping point and the ground under her feet was like quicksand. One minute she had been on solid ground and then, in the blink of an eye, her sister was on her doorstep, Ryan was in her house breaking down her fortifications just by being there, and she was struggling in quicksand. 'And you, Jess, need to go to bed.'

'I'm not a kid any longer!'

'You behave like one.' In terms of condemnation, it was the first time Jamie had ever taken such a dramatic step. She had been conditioned to look after Jessica, to treat her like a baby, to make sure that her needs were met because she, Jamie, was the stronger one, the older one, the one upon whom the responsibilities lay.

In the tense silence that followed her flat statement,

Jessica hesitated, confused, then her lips pursed and she glared sulkily at her sister.

'You can't make me go back up to Scotland, you know,' she muttered.

'We can discuss this in the morning, Jess,' Jamie said wearily. 'I think I've had enough stress today.'

'And she *is* stressed.' Ryan inserted himself into the conversation and Jessica sidled a little closer to him, her body language advertising her interest in a way no amount of words could have done. 'She arrived late for work this morning.'

Jessica giggled and looked at her sister slyly. 'If you'd told me that you were running late, I would have got off the phone sooner. I know you're a stickler for punctuality. Don't worry. I'll be good as gold while I'm here, and you can be the perfect little secretary again and get in to work on time. Mind you...' She looked at Ryan coyly. 'If I had a boss like this one, I'd be getting in to work at six and leaving at midnight. Or maybe not leaving at all...'

Jamie turned on her heels and stalked off towards the kitchen. She knew how these conversations with her sister went. The slightest whiff of criticism and she would react with jibes below the belt that were designed to wound. Jamie had long discovered that the fastest way of dealing with this was to walk away from the situation, to treat her sister like a child who was not responsible for her tantrums. They blew over as quickly as they materialised and making herself scarce removed her from the eye of the storm.

She half-expected Jessica to linger on the staircase, turning on the full-wattage smile and bringing all her feminine wiles to play in an effort to charm Ryan. But, in fact, barely had Jamie sat at the kitchen table than Ryan appeared in the doorway and looked at her quietly, his hands shoved into his pockets.

An uncomfortable silence gathered around them which she broke by reluctantly offering him a cup of coffee.

She would cheerfully have sent him on his way, but there were things that needed to be said, and, reluctant as she was to open up any kind of discussion on her private life, she had no idea how she could avoid the issue.

'Where's Jessica?' she asked, standing up and moving across to the kettle.

'I sent her on her way.'

'And she listened?'

'I have that way with women.'

Jamie snorted, no longer bothering with the niceties that would have been more appropriate given that he was the guy who paid her salary. He had invaded her territory, and as far as she was concerned niceties were temporarily suspended.

'Now you know why I got in late to work this morning. Jessica kept me on the phone for nearly an hour. She was a mess. I only knew that she had decided to sort herself out by coming down here when she phoned me from the train.'

'No big deal.' Ryan took the mug she was holding out to him and sat down. 'Family crises happen. Why didn't you just tell me the truth this morning?' He watched her and realised that she was barely seeing him as she walked towards the kitchen table, nursing the mug in her hands. For a man who was fully aware of the impact he had on the opposite sex, being rendered invisible was a new experience.

He, on the other hand, keenly noted this new casual dress-code of hers, the one she used when she wasn't wearing her work hat. Lazy eyes took in the way her jeans clung to a body that curved in all the right places and the way her long-sleeved tee-shirt skimmed a flat stomach and lovingly contoured pert, full breasts. Even her hair looked different—less neat and pristine, more tousled, as though she had spent time running her fingers through it. Which, judging from what he had picked up of the atmosphere in the house so far, she probably had.

'I suppose because I happen to think that what happens in my private life is no business of yours.'

'Oh, for God's sake, I didn't even know that you had a sister! How much of a state secret could that possibly be?'

Jamie flushed and fiddled with the mug before taking a sip of coffee. 'I...I'm not really the confiding type.'

'Really? I'd never have guessed.'

'I didn't tell you about Jessica because the chances of you ever running into her were non-existent. I live in London, she lives just outside Edinburgh. She isn't a part of my daily life.'

'And that was exactly the way you wanted it until she had the misfortune to need your support.'

'Please don't presume to have any insight at all into my family affairs!'

'If you don't want me to presume, then you're going to have to be a bit more forthcoming.'

'Why? What difference does it make? I do a very good job for you and that's all that matters.'

'Why are you so uncomfortable with this conversation?' He could have let it go. She was right; she delivered the goods when it came to her job and whatever happened outside it was absolutely none of his business. But Ryan decided that he didn't want to let it go. It was as though a door had been partially opened and what lay behind it promised to be so intriguing that he was compelled to try and push the door a little wider.

'You don't understand. You're my boss, for a start, and like I said I'm not into confiding. I prefer to keep my own counsel. Maybe it's a reaction to having a sister like Jess. She always made so much noise that it was just a lot easier to keep quiet and let her get on with it.'

'Easier, but maybe not better. Forget for a minute that I'm your boss. Pretend that I'm just anybody—your next-door neighbour who has come over to borrow a cup of sugar, co-incidentally just at a time when you need a shoulder to cry on...'

'I'm supposed to think of you as my next-door neighbour on the scrounge for a cup of sugar?' She was momentarily distracted enough by the image to feel her lips twitch. 'What would you be doing with the cup of sugar?'

'Baking a cake, because I happen to be a kindly and caring neighbour who enjoys baking. It's my favourite pastime. Next to flower arranging and cross stitch.' She was relaxing. She was even smiling and he felt a kick of gratification that he had been responsible for that. For some reason, he didn't care for the idea of her stressed out, tearful and unable to talk to anyone about it. His experience of women was that they couldn't wait to pour their hearts out and confide in whomsoever happened to be willing to listen. He was the youngest of four and the only boy in the family. He could remember many an instance of sitting out one of his sister's ridiculously long phone calls, waiting impatiently to use the telephone.

This level of reticence was new to him. 'So...?' he prompted encouragingly.

'So, look, I'm not sure how to say this but...' Jamie sighed and adopted a slightly different approach. 'Now that you've met my sister, what do you think of her?'

'After all of my five-second acquaintance, I'm only qualified to tell you that she's very attractive.'

Jamie felt a stab of disappointment but she nodded sagely at him. 'She's always been the prettier one.'

'Hang on a minute...'

'Spare me the kindness. I'm stating a fact, and it's not something that's ever bothered me anyway.' But for a fleeting second Jamie wondered what he had been about to say. Of course, it would have been a polite lie, but nevertheless... 'Jessica's beautiful and she knows it. She's also married and going through a bit of a bad patch which will blow over just so long as...'

'As she's not offered any distractions by someone like me?' He looked at her coolly.

'I know what type of girls you go for—tall, blonde, beautiful and pliable. Well, Jess is tall, blonde, beautiful and at the moment she happens to be very pliable. I know you probably think that I'm being totally out of order in saying this stuff, but you chose to come here, and now that you're here I'm afraid I have every right to say what's on my mind.' She licked her lips nervously. 'I hope I'm not jeopardising my job by telling you this.'

'Jeopardising your job? What kind of person do you think I am?' He was outraged to think that she could even consider him the type of man who would penalise her for speaking her mind. Was that what she thought of him? Under her cool, dutiful exterior, did she think that he was some sort of monster?

'Don't worry, your job is perfectly safe, and if you're so obsessive about your privacy then I'm happy to walk out that door right now and leave you to get on with hiding behind your walls. As for your sister, she might be the sort of woman I date, but I don't date married women, even married women who claim to be unhappily married.'

He stood up and the colour drained from Jamie's face. She had enjoyed the free and easy way he had always had with her. It was all part and parcel of his unconventional personality, that curious, alluring mix of creativity, intelligence and self-assurance. Did she want to lose that? Did she want a boss who stuck to the rules and never teased her, or over-stepped the boundaries in asking about her personal life? That thought left her cold and she hurriedly got to her feet and reached out to put a restraining hand on his arm.

'I'm sorry. I know how that sounded, but I have to look out for my sister. You see…' She hesitated a fraction of a second. 'Our dad died when I was six, and when Jess was sixteen Mum died after complications following an operation. It was horrible. I was left in charge. Mum made me promise that I would look after her. I was about to go to university, but I found myself having to get a job and look after Jess.'

'That was a lot of responsibility for someone so young,' Ryan murmured, sitting back down.

'It wasn't easy,' Jamie agreed. 'Jess was boy crazy and I nearly tore my hair out making sure she showed up at school every day and left with a handful of qualifications.'

'What were you doing for a job?' he asked curiously, and was even more curious when slow colour crept into her cheeks and she looked down.

'Oh, just working at a vet's. It wasn't what I had expected to be doing at the age of nineteen, but I enjoyed it. The thing is…'

'What had you expected to be doing?'

'Huh?'

'Your plans? Dreams? Ambitions? What were they before your life was derailed?'

'Well…' Jamie flushed and hesitated. 'I wanted to go to university and study law. Seems like a lifetime ago! Anyway, that's not important. The important thing is that I just wanted to warn you off her.'

'Tough, having to give up on your dreams. There must be a part of you that resents her.'

'Of course there isn't! No one can help what life throws at them.'

'Noble sentiment. Alas, not many of us are noble creatures.'

'As I was saying…' Jamie chose to ignore the invitation to elaborate. 'I just wanted to warn you off her.'

'Because she's going to dutifully return to her husband and they're both going to live happily ever after?'

'Yes!'

'Warning duly noted.'

'What warning?'

Jessica was standing in the doorway of the kitchen, and with a sinking heart Jamie realised that she hadn't vanished because she had been instructed to vanish—she had vanished so that she could have a shower and resurface in the least amount of clothing possible. She was kitted out in slinky lounging culottes and a tiny vest, worn bra-less, that left nothing to the imagination. She had a stupendous figure and every inch of it was available for inspection as she walked slowly into the kitchen, enjoying the attention.

Through the thin, grey vest, Jamie could see the outline of her sister's nipples. Ryan would similarly be taking that in. Yes, he had told her that he would keep away from Jessica, but how strong was any red-blooded man's will power when it came to a sexy woman who was overtly encouraging?

'Well?' Jessica paused and leaned against the counter, legs lightly crossed at the ankles, her back arched so that her breasts were provocatively thrust forward. 'What warning?'

'A warning,' Ryan drawled, 'that I'm not to interfere and try and persuade you to return to your husband.'

Jessica looked at her sister narrowly. 'That true, Jamie?'

'Why would he lie?'

'So you don't mind me staying with you for a while? Maybe until Christmas is over? I mean, it's only a couple of weeks away. I could help you decorate the tree and stuff and by then I might have got my head together.'

Boxed in, Jamie had no choice but to concede defeat.

'Hey, we could even have a party!' She looked sideways at Ryan and shot him a half-smile. 'I'm great at organising parties. What are *you* up to at Christmas, anyway?'

'Jessica!'

'Oh, don't be such a bore, Jamie.'

'I'm in the country,' Ryan murmured. 'Why?' He had already received so many invitations to join people for Christmas lunch that he was seriously considering ignoring them all and locking himself away in his apartment until the fuss was over.

'You could join us here.'

Adjacent to Jamie, he was aware of her look of pure horror at the suggestion. He nearly burst out laughing, but he managed to keep a straight face as he appeared to give the offer considerable thought.

'Well…' He hesitated. 'I am in the unique position of spending Christmas day without my family.'

'Where are they?' Jessica strolled towards him, her thumbs hooked lightly into the elasticated waistband of the culottes so that they were dragged slightly down, exposing a flat, brown belly and the twinkling glitter of her pierced navel.

No wonder Jamie worried about her sister, Ryan thought. The woman was clearly a walking, talking liability to anybody's peace of mind.

'They're in the Caribbean.'

Jessica's eyes rounded into impressed saucers and her mouth fell open. 'You're kidding.'

'I have a house there and this year they've all decided to spend Christmas and New Year in it.'

'I don't know why we're having this silly conversation,'

Jamie interrupted crisply. 'Ryan already has his own plans for Christmas.' She rose to her feet and pulled open the dishwasher, which was her way of announcing that it was time for the impromptu evening to come to an end. But Jessica was in full flow, quizzing Ryan about his house in the Caribbean, asking him what it looked like, while he answered with just the sort of indulgent amusement that she was accustomed to getting. It had never mattered what boundaries Jessica had over-stepped; the world had always smiled and allowed her to get away with it. Whoever said that beautiful people didn't lead charmed lives?

'I'm open to persuasion,' Ryan finished, leaning back and watching Jamie bang pans into cupboards, frustration stamped on her face, her mouth downturned and scowling. 'What were *you* going to do, Jamie? Bit boring if you had been planning to stay in on your own.'

'I would rather call it peaceful,' she snapped. 'And, besides, I had plans to go out for drinks on Christmas morning with some friends and I would probably have hung around for their alternative Christmas lunch.'

'I want traditional,' Jessica stated flatly.

'What's Greg going to do?' Jamie spun round to look at her sister. 'Does he know that you're planning on abandoning him for Christmas day?'

'He won't mind. He's on call, and anyway, his parents can't wait to have him all to themselves so that they can tell him what a rotten wife I am. So...' That technicality concluded, Jessica turned her attention back to Ryan, who looked as comfortable and settled in the kitchen as though he had been there a million times. 'Will you come? Jamie's never been into Christmas, but I'll make her stick up a tree, and it'll be festive with a turkey and all the trimmings!'

'I'm sure he'll think about it. Just stop nagging him, Jess!' Jamie was pretty sure that she could convince Ryan to ignore her sister's rantings. He was a guy who was in great demand. The last thing he would want to do would be to sit around a small pine table in a kitchen and dine on a turkey reluctantly cooked by his secretary. Just the thought of it made her shiver in nervous apprehension.

'It's wonderful the way you can answer on my behalf.' Ryan grinned at Jamie, who scowled back at him. 'It's probably why we work so well together. You know just when to read my mind.'

'Ha-ha. Very funny.'

'But she's right.' He stood up and glanced at Jessica. 'I'll think about it and let Jamie know.'

'Or you could let me know. I'll give you my mobile number and you can get in touch any time at all. No need to go through Jamie.'

He left five minutes later and Jamie sagged. The peace of having her sister upstairs safely in bed was greatly diminished by the nasty tangle of thoughts playing in her mind.

Not only had Ryan found out more about her in the space of an hour than he had in eighteen months, but she was now facing the alarming prospect that, having wedged his foot through the door, it would be impossible to get him to remove it.

Everything that had always been so straightforward had now been turned on its head.

And what if the man decided to descend on them for Christmas lunch?

Apprehension sizzled in her and, alongside that very natural apprehension, something else, something even more worrying, something that closely resembled…anticipation.

CHAPTER THREE

CHRISTMAS'S rapid approach brought a temporary lull in the usual relentless work-ethic. Ryan Sheppard made a very good Christmas boss. He entered into the spirit of things by personally supervising the decorations and cracking open champagne at six every evening for whoever happened to be around in the countdown to the big day. Extra-long lunch hours shopping were tactfully overlooked. On Christmas Eve, work was due to stop at twelve and the rest of the day given over to the Secret Santa gift exchanges and an elaborate buffet lunch which would be prepared by Ryan's caterers.

On the home front, Jamie was stoically putting up with a sister who had decided to throw herself into the party season with gay abandon. She tagged along to all the Christmas parties to which Jamie had been invited, flirted outrageously with every halfway decent-looking bachelor, and in the space of a week and a half collected more phone numbers than Jamie had in her address book. There was, ominously, no mention of Greg. If they were in contact, it certainly wasn't via the landline. Jamie had stopped asking because the response of tear-filled eyes, followed by an angry sermon about the valuable space for which she was still searching, was just too much of a headache.

A tree had been erected and Jessica had enthusiastically

begun helping with the lights, but like a child, had become bored after fifteen minutes, leaving Jamie to complete the task. Clothes were left strewn in unlikely places and were retrieved with an air of self-sacrifice whenever Jamie happened to mention the state of the house. The consequence of this was that Jamie's peaceful existence was now a round-the-clock chore of tidying up behind her sister and nagging.

Of course, Jamie knew that she would have to sit her sister down and insist on knowing when she intended to return to Scotland, but like a coward she hid behind the Christmas chaos and decided to shelve all delicate discussions until Boxing Day at the very least.

There was also the hurdle of Christmas day to get through. Ryan had, totally unexpectedly, accepted Jessica's foolish invitation to lunch and, with the prospect of three people cutting into a turkey that would be way too big, Jamie had invited several other members of staff to come along if they weren't doing anything.

Three guys from the software department had taken her up on the invitation, as well as a couple of her girlfriends whom she had met at the gym when she had first arrived in London.

Jamie anticipated an awkward lunch, but when she mentioned that to her sister, Jessica had smiled brightly and assured her that there was no need to worry.

'I'm a party animal!' she had announced. 'I can make any gathering go with a bang, and I've got loads of party hats and crackers and stuff. It'll be a blast! So much better than last year, which was a deadly meal round at the in-laws'. I can't wait to fill Greg in when the last guest leaves.'

'I'm surprised you even care what he thinks,' Jamie had said and was vaguely reassured when her sister had gone bright red.

Not that she had dwelled on that for any length of time.

Most of her mind for the past week had been taken up with the prospect of Ryan descending on her house for Christmas lunch.

And now the day had finally arrived. It came with dark, leaden skies and a general feeling of anticlimax; although some snow had been forecast, it appeared to be in the process of falling everywhere else but in London.

From downstairs came the thud of music, a compilation of songs which Jessica had prepared during her spare time. Peace seemed a distant dream. At eight-thirty, Jamie had thoroughly cleaned the bathroom, which had been taken over by her sister in a series of undercover assaults, so that each day slightly more appeared on the shelf and in the cabinet.

Now, sitting and staring at her reflection in the mirror, Jamie wondered how much longer she would be able to cope with a very hyper Jessica.

Then she thought about her outfit: a long-sleeved black dress that, she knew, would look drab against the peacock-blue of Jessica's mini skirt and her high wedges that would escalate her height to six feet.

By the time the first guest arrived, Jamie was already settling into her role of background assistant to her life-and-soul-of-the-party sister.

Every nerve in her body was tuned to the sound of the doorbell, but when Ryan eventually appeared, she was in the kitchen, as it happened, doing various things with the meal. Outside alcohol was steadily being consumed and Jessica was flirting, dancing and enjoying the limelight, even though the guys concerned were the sort of highly intelligent eccentrics she would ordinarily have dismissed as complete nerds.

The sound of his voice behind her, lazy and amused, zapped her like a bolt of live electricity and she leapt to her feet and spun around, having been peering worriedly into the oven.

'Well,' he drawled, walking into the kitchen and peering underneath lids at the food sitting on the counter, 'looks like the party's going with a swing.'

'You're here.'

'Did you think that I wasn't going to turn up?' Since the last time he had seen her in jeans and a tee-shirt, he had found himself doing quite a bit of thinking about her. As expected, she had mentioned nothing about her sister when she had been at work, which didn't mean that their working relationship had remained the same. It hadn't. Something subtle had altered, although he had a feeling that that just applied to him. She had been as efficient, as distant and as perfectly polite as ever.

'I'm nothing if not one-hundred-percent reliable.' He held out a carrier bag. 'Champagne.'

Flustered, she kept her eyes firmly on his face, deliberately avoiding the muscular legs encased in pair of black trousers and the way those top two undone buttons of his cream shirt exposed the shadow of fine, dark hair.

'Thanks.' She reached out for the carrier bag and was startled when from behind his back he produced a small gift-wrapped box. 'What's this?'

'A present.'

'I'm still working my way through the bottle of perfume you gave me last year.' She wiped her hands and then began opening the present.

Her mouth went dry. She had been privy to quite a few of his gifts to women. They ranged from extravagant bouquets of flowers to jewellery to trips to health spas. This, however, was nothing like that. In the small box was an antique butterfly brooch and she picked it up, held it up to the light and then set it back down in its bed of tissue paper before raising her eyes to his.

'You bought me a butterfly,' she whispered.

'I noticed that you had a few on your mantelpiece in the sitting room. I guessed you collect them. I found this one at an antique shop in Spitalfields.'

'It's beautiful, but I can't accept it.' She thrust it at him and turned away, her face burning.

'Why not?'

'Because…because…'

'Because you don't collect them?'

'I do, but…'

'But it's yet another of those secrets of yours that you'd rather I knew nothing about?'

'It just isn't appropriate,' Jamie told him stiffly. In her head, she pictured him roaming through a market, chancing upon the one thing he knew would appeal to her, handing over not a great deal of cash for it, but it never took much to win someone over. Except, she wasn't on the market to be won over. Nor was he on the market for doing anything but what came naturally to him—thinking outside the box. It was why he was such a tremendous success in his field.

'Okay, but you know that it's an insult to return a gift.' Ryan shrugged. 'I'm in your house. Consider it a small token of gratitude for rescuing a lonely soul from wandering the streets of London on Christmas day.'

'Oh, please.' Her breathing was shallow and she was painfully conscious of the fact that whilst outside the music was blaring, probably getting on the neighbours' nerves, inside the kitchen it was just the two of them locked in a strange intimacy that terrified her.

This was not what she wanted. She urgently reminded herself of Greg and her foolish love-sick infatuation with him before Jessica had arrived on the scene and stolen his heart.

But to insist on returning the brooch would risk making just too big a deal of it. It would alert him to the fact that for some reason his gesture bothered her.

'I haven't got anything for you,' she said uncomfortably.

'I'll live with that. Why butterflies?'

'My father was keen on them,' Jamie said awkwardly as another piece of information left her and travelled across to him. 'Mum told us a lot about him. He loved to travel. He particularly loved to travel to study insects, and out of all the insects butterflies interested him most. He liked the fact that there were so many different varieties of them and they came in so many different colours and shapes and sizes. Mum said that he figured they were a lot more interesting than the human species.'

Her voice and expression had softened as she lost herself in a memory that hadn't surfaced for years. 'So I started collecting them when I was a kid. I just keep the better ones on show, but I have a box upstairs full of silly plastic ones I had when I was growing up.' A sudden blast of music hit her as the kitchen door was pushed open and the moment of crazy reminiscing was lost with the appearance of Jessica, now wearing a shiny party hat and with her arm around one of the computer geeks, who looked thrilled to death with the leggy blonde clinging to him.

'Enjoy the attention, buddy.' Ryan grinned at his top software-specialist. 'But bear in mind the lady's married.'

Outside, the party of six guests had swelled to ten. Jessica had asked a couple of others 'to liven things up'. Bottles of wine were ranged on the sideboard in the living room and the chairs had been cleared away to create a dance floor of sorts.

Walking into the room was like walking into a disco, but

one where the decor was comprised of a Christmas tree in the corner and random decorations strung along the walls. In the centre of it all, Jessica was living up to her reputation as a party animal.

Swaying to the music with a drink in one hand and her eyes half-closed, she was the peacock, proud of her stupendous figure, which outranked even those of the gym queens at the side, and the cynosure of all male eyes.

When the beat went from fast to slow, Jamie looked away as Jessica draped herself over Ryan.

So what else had she expected? That he would actually be able to resist the allure of an available woman? A dull ache began in her head. She mingled and chatted and even half-heartedly danced with her colleague Robbie who charmed her with an enthusiastic conversation about something he was working on at the moment, something guaranteed to be bigger and better than anything else on the market.

While Ryan danced on with Jessica.

Several of the neighbours began popping in, drawn by the music. On either side, they were young, professional couples whom Jamie had glimpsed in passing. Now, she realised that they were people with whom she could easily become friendly, and the distraction was a blessing. It took her out of the living room and into the kitchen, where they congregated and compared notes on the neighbourhood.

She wasn't too sure how the matter of eating was going to be achieved. As expected, the bulk of the preparations had been left to her while her sister had stalked ineffectively around the kitchen with a glass of wine in her hand, sighing and making useless suggestions about what could be done to speed up the whole process. 'Dump the lot and order in a Chinese', had been one of her more ridiculous offerings, especially considering she had been the one to insist on the full turkey extravaganza.

Flushed from the heat in the kitchen, and nursing enough low-level resentment to sink a small ship, Jamie was fetching the wretched turkey out of the oven when Ryan's voice behind her nearly made her drop the hapless bird.

'You need a hand.'

Jamie carefully deposited the aluminium baking dish on the counter and glanced across to him.

'I'm fine. Thank you.'

'Just stating the obvious here, but martyrs aren't known to be the happiest people on the face of the earth.'

'I'm not being a martyr!' She turned to look at him, hacked off and grim. 'I was coerced into doing...*this*.' A sweeping gesture encompassed the kitchen, which looked as though it had been the target of a small explosion. 'So I'm doing it.'

'Exactly—you're being a martyr. If you didn't want to do all...*this*—' he mirrored her sweeping gesture '—then you shouldn't have.'

'Do you have any idea what my sister's like when she doesn't manage to get her own way?' Jamie cried with a hint of hysteria in her voice. 'Oh, no, of course you don't, because *you* haven't had years of her! Because *you* are only being shown the smiling, sexy side that leaves men breathless and panting.'

'My breathing's perfectly normal.' He rescued the potatoes and began searching around for other dishes, into which he began piling the food. 'Look, why don't you go and drag your sister in here and force her to give you a helping hand?'

Jamie opened her mouth to tell him just how silly his suggestion was—because Jessica never, but *never*, did anything she didn't want to do—and instead sighed wryly.

'That would come under the heading of "mission impossible".'

'In that case, I'm helping, whether you like it or not.'

'You're my boss. You're not supposed to be in here helping.'

'You're right, I am your boss—you are therefore obliged to do whatever I ask.'

Jamie couldn't help it. She went bright red at the unintended innuendo and was mortified when Ryan burst out laughing.

'Within reason, of course...' He raised his eyebrows in amusement. 'Although I gather from your sister that there wouldn't be any outraged boyfriend threatening to break my kneecaps if I decided to push the point...'

He was still grinning. *Laughing* at her. She turned away abruptly, knowing that the back of her neck was giveaway-red and that her hands were shaking as she poured gravy into the gravy boat and busied herself with the roast potatoes.

'Jessica shouldn't be talking about my private life!' she managed, on the verge of tears. Tears of pure frustration.

'She said that you didn't have a boyfriend,' Ryan said mildly. 'What's the big deal?'

'The *big deal* is that it's none of your business!'

'You know, it's dangerous to be so secretive. Makes other people even more intrigued.'

'There's nothing intriguing about my private life,' Jamie snapped. 'It's not nearly as glamorous or adventurous as *yours*.'

'If you really thought that my life was glamorous, exciting and adventurous, then you wouldn't be so disapproving—and don't deny that you disapprove. You admitted it yourself—you think I'm an unscrupulous womaniser with no morals.'

'I never said that!' She met his amused grin with a reluctant smile of her own. 'Okay, maybe I implied that you... Why are you being difficult, Ryan Sheppard?'

'What an outrageous accusation, Jamie Powell,' Ryan said piously. 'No one likes being accused of being exciting and adventurous.'

'I never said that. You're twisting my words.'

'You know, you may not be obvious in the way that your sister is, but when it comes to getting a man—and believe me, I know what I'm talking about—you have...'

'Stop! I don't want to hear what you're going to say.'

'Somehow, over the years, your sister has managed to destroy your self-confidence.'

'I have plenty of self-confidence. I work with you. You should know that.'

'Yes, you certainly do when it comes to the work front, but on an emotional level let's just say that I'm beginning to see you for the first time.' *And liking what I see*, he could have added.

Jamie didn't like the sound of that. She also didn't like the way his throwaway remarks were making her question herself. *Was* she lacking in self-confidence? Was he implying that she was emotionally stunted?

'You *were* going to help, or at least that's what you said. You never mentioned that you were going to play amateur psychologist. So can you get the plastic cups from the cupboard over here, and stop giving me lots of homespun advice? And I don't,' she burst out, unable to contain herself, 'have a boyfriend because I've never seen the need to grab anything that's available because it's better than nothing at all!'

She found that they were suddenly staring at each other with the music outside—a dull, steady throb—and the aromatic smells in the hot kitchen swirling around them like a seductive, heady incense.

'Good policy,' Ryan murmured, taking in the patches of heightened colour in her cheeks and the way her eyes glittered—nothing like the cool, composed woman he was so accustomed to working alongside.

'And if I *did* have a man in my life,' she heard herself continue, with horror, 'he certainly wouldn't be the sort of person who runs around breaking other people's kneecaps.'

'Because you can take care of yourself.'

'Exactly!'

'And you definitely wouldn't be drawn to a caveman.'

'No, I wouldn't.'

'So what *would* you be drawn to?'

'Thoughtful. Sensitive. Caring.' With sudden alarm, she realised that somewhere along the line she had breached her own defences and allowed emotion to take control over her careful reserve.

But she had just been so mad. After the nightmare challenge of having to cope with her sister landing on her doorstep with her uninvited emotional baggage, and the chaos of having to deal with a Christmas lunch that had been foisted upon her, the thought of Jessica getting drunk and gossiping about her behind her back to her boss had been too much.

'I'm sorry,' she apologised stiffly, turning away and gathering herself.

Not so fast, Ryan wanted to say, *not when you've set my mind whirring.*

'For what?' As in the office, they seemed to work well together in the kitchen, with Jamie dealing with the food while Ryan efficiently piled the dirty dishes into the sink. 'For happening to have feelings?'

'There's a time and a place for everything.' Her voice was definitely back in full working order; frankly, if he chose to snigger at her behind her back at her woefully single state, then that was his prerogative. 'My kitchen on Christmas day definitely isn't either.'

'We could always alter the time and the venue. Like I

said, it's important for a boss to know what's going on in his secretary's life.'

'No. It isn't.' But of course he was teasing her and she half smiled, pleased that the normal order was restored.

Watching her, Ryan felt a sudden kick of annoyance. Would he have taken her out, maybe for dinner, in an attempt to prise beneath that smooth exterior? He didn't know, but he did realise that she was quietly and efficiently re-erecting her barriers.

Oozing sympathy, he turned her to face him, his hands resting lightly on her shoulders. 'People tell me that I'm a terrific listener,' he murmured persuasively. 'And I pride myself on being able to read other people.'

Jamie opened her mouth to utter something polite but sarcastic, and instead found herself dry-mouthed and blinking owl-like as he stared down at her. He really was sinfully, shamefully beautiful, she thought, dazed.

'And I didn't mean to offend you by suggesting that your outgoing, in-your-face sister might have been ruinous on your levels of self-confidence. I'm just guessing that you've been messed up in the past.'

'What are you talking about?' she whispered.

'Some loser broke your heart and you haven't been able to move on.'

Jamie drew her breath in sharply and pulled away from him, breaking the mesmeric spell he had temporarily cast over her. She pressed herself against the kitchen counter, hands behind her back.

'What did my sister say to you?'

Ryan had been fishing in the dark. He had been curious—understandably curious, he thought. In his world, women were an open book. It was refreshing to be challenged with one who wasn't. Now, he felt like the angler who, against all odds, has managed to land a fish.

She was as white as a sheet, and although she was trying hard to maintain a semblance of composure he knew that it was a struggle.

So who the hell was the guy who had broken her heart?

'This is ridiculous!' Abruptly, Jamie turned away and began gathering a stack of plates in her hands. They were all disposable paper plates because there was no way that she would be left standing by the sink after the last guest had departed, washing dishes while her sister retired to bed for some well-deserved sleep after copious alcohol consumption.

'Trust me, he wasn't worth it.' Ryan was enraged on her behalf.

'I really don't want to talk about this.'

'Sometimes those caring, sharing types can prove to be the biggest bastards on the face of the earth.'

'How would *you* know?' She spun round to look at him with flashing eyes. 'For your information, the caring, sharing guy in question was the nicest man I've ever met.'

'Not that nice, if he trampled over you. What was it? Was he married? Stringing you along by pretending he was single and unattached? Or maybe promising to dump his wife who didn't understand him? Or was he seeing other women on the side? Underneath that caring, sharing exterior, was he living it up behind your back—was that it? Word of advice here—men who get a tear in their eye during sad movies and insist on cooking for you because they get home at five every evening don't necessarily have the monopoly on the moral high-ground. You've got to let it go, Jamie.'

'Let it go and start doing *what*?' she heard herself asking as she gripped the paper plates in her hand.

'Join the dating scene.'

'So that I can…?'

'Finish what you were going to say.' Ryan moved to block

her exit. 'Like I said, there's never any need for you to think that you can't speak freely to me. We're not in a work environment here. Say whatever you want to say.'

'Okay, here's what I want to say—whatever hang-ups I have, there's no way I would join any dating scene if there was a possibility of bumping into men like you, Ryan Sheppard!'

Ryan's lips thinned. She was skating dangerously close to thin ice but hadn't he invited her to be frank and open with him? Hadn't he insisted? On the other hand, he hadn't expected her to throw his kindness back in his face. He was giving her the benefit of his experience, warning her of the perils of the sort of smiley, happy jerk she claimed to like, providing her with a shoulder to cry on—and in return...?

'Men *like me*?' he enquired coldly.

'Sorry, but you did ask me to be honest.'

Ryan forced himself to offer her a smile. 'I don't lead women up the garden path and break their hearts,' he gritted.

'No one led me up a garden path!' But she had said too much. She was hot, bothered and flustered and regretting every mis-spoken word. 'We should get this food out there before it all goes stone cold,' she carried on.

'In other words, you want this conversation terminated.'

Jamie avoided his eyes and maintained a mute silence. 'I apologise if I said certain things that you might construe as insulting,' she eventually offered in a stilted voice, and he scowled. 'And I'd appreciate it if we could just leave it here and not mention this conversation again.'

'And what if I don't agree to that?'

Jamie looked at him calmly, composure regained, but at a very high cost to her treasured peace of mind. 'I don't think I could work happily alongside you otherwise. I'm a very private person and it would be impossible for me to function if I feared that you might start...' *Finding my life a subject for conjecture.*

'Start what?'

'Trying to get under my skin because you find it amusing.'

Her eyes weren't quite brown, Ryan caught himself thinking. There were flecks of green and gold there that he had never noticed before. But then again, why would he have noticed, when she kept her eyes studiously averted from his face most of the time?

He stood aside with ill humour and pushed open the door for her and immediately they were assailed with the sound of raised voices and laughter. While they had been in the kitchen, a cabaret had obviously been going on and, sure enough, Jessica had pulled one of the tables to the side of the room and was doing her best to hang some mistletoe from the light on the ceiling in the middle of the room, while surrounded by a circle of guests who were clearly enjoying the spectacle.

Food was greeted with clapping and cheering. The neighbours made a half-hearted attempt to head back to their houses, but were easily persuaded to stay. All hands hit the deck and more drink surfaced while, to one side, Jamie watched proceedings. And Ryan watched Jamie, out of the corner of his eye. Watched as she pretended to join in, although her smile was strained whenever she looked across to her flamboyant sister. Surrounded by an audience, Jessica was like one of the glittering baubles on the Christmas tree.

It was nearly five-thirty by the time the food had been depleted and Jamie began the laborious process of clearing.

Exhaustion felt like lead weights around her ankles and she knew that her tiredness had nothing to do with the task of making Christmas lunch. It was of the mental variety and that was a much more difficult prospect to shake off.

Talking to Ryan in the kitchen, exploding in front of him like an unpredictable hand grenade, had drained her and she knew why.

For the first time in her life, she had allowed herself to let go. The result had been terrifying and if she could only have taken it all back then she would have.

Sneaking a glance to her right, she looked at him. He had dutifully helped clear away dishes, along with everyone else minus her sister, and now he was laughing and joking with the guys from his office. Doubtless he had completely forgotten their conversation, while she…

She watched as, giggling and swaying her hips to the rhythm of the music, Jessica began beckoning him across to where she had positioned herself neatly underneath the precariously hanging bunch of mistletoe.

Ryan looked far from thrilled at the situation and for once Jamie was not going to rush in and try and save her sister from herself. If Jessica wanted to fool around in her quest to find herself, then so be it. Jamie had spent a lifetime standing behind her, desperately attempting to rescue her from her own waywardness.

Lord, in the process she had even forgotten how to take care of her own emotional needs! She had bottled everything up; how pathetic was it that the one time she actually managed to release the cork on that bottle it was with her boss, the least appropriate or suitable person when it came to shoulder-lending! He went through women like water and had probably never had a decent conversation of any depth with any of the bimbos who clung to him like superglue. Yet she had directed all her angst at him—in an unstoppable stream of admissions that she knew she would eternally live to regret.

She was turning away, heading for the sanctuary of the kitchen, when she happened to glance through the window.

No one had bothered to draw the curtains and there, stepping out of his car—the same old battered Land Rover which he had had ever since she had first started working for him—was her brother-in-law.

For a few seconds, Jamie could scarcely believe her eyes. She hadn't seen Greg for absolutely ages. She had fled with her pride and dignity intact, determined to keep her love for him firmly under wraps while he got on with the business of showering Jessica with his devotion. Since then, she hadn't trusted herself to be anywhere near him, because she would rather have died than to let her secret leap out of its box.

The years hadn't changed him. He was turning now to slot his key into the lock; everything about him was surprisingly the same. His fair hair still flopped over his eyes and he still carried himself with the same lanky awkwardness that Jamie had once found so incredibly endearing. She could make all that out even under the unsatisfactory street lighting.

She peeled her eyes away for a fraction of a second to see Jessica reaching out to put her hands on Ryan's shoulders. In a second, Jamie thought with a surge of panic two things would happen: Greg would turn around and look straight through the window, and Jessica would close her eyes and plant a very public kiss on Ryan's mouth.

Galvanised, she sprinted across the room. If she had had time to think about it, she wasn't sure whether she would have followed through, but as it was she acted purely on instinct, fired by a driving need to make sure that her sister didn't completely blow the one chance she had in life of true happiness—because Greg was as good as it would ever get for Jessica.

She pulled Ryan around and saw his surprise mingled with relief to have been spared the embarrassment of having to gently but firmly turn Jessica away. Janie reached up and curled her hand around his neck, and even at the height of her spontaneity she was stomach clenchingly aware of the muscularity of his body.

'Wha...?'

'Mistletoe!' Jamie stated. 'We're under it. So we'd better do what tradition demands.'

Ryan laughed softly under his breath and curved his hand around her waist.

As far as days went, this one was turning out to be full of unexpected twists and turns; he couldn't remember enjoying himself so much for a very long time indeed.

He didn't know what had brought about this change in Jamie but he liked it. He especially liked the feel of her body as it softened against his. He felt her breasts push against his chest. She smelled of something clean and slightly floral and her full mouth was parted, her eyes half-closed. It was the most seductive thing he had ever experienced in his life.

Who was he to resist? He gathered her to him and kissed her, a long, deep kiss that started soft and slow and increased tempo until he was losing himself in it, not caring if they were spectator sport.

He surfaced when she twisted out of his arms and turned around. Reluctantly, Ryan followed her gaze, as did everyone else in the room, to the blond-haired man standing in the doorway with an overnight bag in one hand and a bunch of straggling flowers in the other.

CHAPTER FOUR

RYAN looked at his watch and scowled. The offices were pretty bare of staff, just the skeleton lot who got more of a kick at work at their computers, creating programmes and testing games, than they did in their own homes.

Not the point.

The point was that it was now ten fifteen and Jamie should have been in one hour and fifteen minutes ago. Christmas day had come and gone. Boxing Day had come and gone. She hadn't booked any holiday time beyond that.

He swung his jean-clad legs off his desk, sending a pile of paperwork to the ground in the process, and stalked across the floor-to-ceiling window so that he could look outside and, bad-tempered, survey the grey, bleak London streets which were eerily quiet in this part of the city.

He was still reeling from the events of Christmas day, much to his enduring annoyance. He had gone to satisfy a simple and one-hundred-percent understandable curiosity and had got the equivalent of a full round in a boxing ring—starting with that little conversation in the kitchen with Jamie, followed by her kissing him and culminating in the appearance of the man at the door.

It had been a comedy in three acts, except Ryan couldn't be further from laughing.

He could still feel the warmth of her mouth against his.

The memory of it had eaten into his Boxing Day, turning him into an ill-tempered guest at the party given by his god-child's parents, a party which had become a tradition of sorts over the years and which he had always enjoyed.

Glancing at his watch again, he was beginning to wonder whether Jamie had decided to jettison work altogether. A week ago such an act of rebellion bordering on mutiny would have been unthinkable, but in the space of a heartbeat all preconceived ideas about his quiet, efficient, scrupulously reserved secretary had been blown to smithereens.

He was in the process of debating whether to call her when his office door was pushed open and there she was, unbuttoning her sensible black coat and tugging at the scarf around her neck.

'This is getting to be a habit,' Ryan grated, striding back to his desk and resuming his position with the chair pushed back and his long legs extended to the side. 'And don't bother to try and tell me stories about delays on the Underground.'

'Okay. I won't.'

Things had irreparably changed. Over a fraught day and a half, Jamie had resigned herself to that and come to the conclusion that the only way she could continue working for Ryan was if she put every single unfortunate personal conversation they had had behind her. Lock them away in a place from where they couldn't affect her working life. And the kiss...

The horror of that moment and the fact that it still clawed away in her mind was something that would have to be locked away as well.

All the same, she was having a hard time meeting his eyes as she relieved herself of her coat, gloves and scarf and deposited the bundle of post on his desk, along with her laptop computer, which she switched on in an increasingly tense silence.

'Look, I'm sorry I'm late,' she eventually said when it seemed like the silence would stretch to infinity. 'It's not going to be a habit, and you know that I'm more than happy to work late tonight to make up for the lost time.'

'I can't have unreliability in my employees—beside the point, whether you're happy to work late or not.'

'Yes, well, I hoped that you might understand given the fact that half the country is still on holiday.' She couldn't prevent the edge of rebelliousness from creeping into her voice, but the past day and a half had been beyond the pale and nothing seemed to be changing. Greg had appeared on the doorstep, putting a swift end to proceedings on Christmas day. Who on earth had been willing to listen to Jessica's histrionics—because her sister had had absolutely no qualms about letting the rest of the world into her problems. Apparently no one. There had been a half-hearted attempt on the part of some to try and clear the sitting room but within forty-five minutes they had all dispersed—including Ryan, although in his case Jamie had had to push him out of the door. In true intrusive style, he had been sharply curious and more than happy to stick around. Jamie was having none of it.

And since then her house, the bastion of her peace of mind, had become the arena for warfare.

Jamie now knew far too much about the state of her sister's marriage for her liking.

With nowhere else to stay, and determined to put things right, Greg had now taken up residence in the sitting room, much to Jessica's disgust. Everything was chaotic and, although Jamie had sat them both down and gently advised them that perhaps sorting out their marriage problems was something that could be better done in their own home, there seemed to be no glimmer of light on the horizon.

Jessica was standing firm about needing her space and

Greg was quietly persistent that he wasn't going to give up on them because she was having a temporary blip.

And now Ryan was sitting stony-faced in front of her and she wasn't sure that she could bear much more.

'Can we get on with some work?' she half pleaded. 'There are a few contracts that you need to look at. I've emailed them to you, and I think Bob Dill has finally completed that software package he's been working on.'

Ryan discovered that he had been waiting to see how things would play out when she showed up for work. Now, it dawned on him that she intended to bury the whole Christmas episode, pretend none of it had ever happened.

He steepled his fingers under his chin and looked at her thoughtfully. 'Yes,' he agreed, tilting his head to one side. 'We certainly could have a look at those contracts, but that's not imperative. Like you said, half the country's still recovering from Christmas.' It was interesting to see the way she flushed at the mention of Christmas. 'Which brings me to the subject of Christmas day.'

'I'd rather we didn't talk about that,' Jamie told him quickly.

'Why not?'

'Because…'

'You find it uncomfortable?'

'Because…' Flustered, Jamie raised her eyes to his and found herself consumed with embarrassing, graphic recall of that kiss they had shared. She had never, in the end, even shared a kiss with Greg. All through that time she had dreamed about him, the closest she had come to actually touching him was on the odd occasion when his hand had accidentally brushed hers or when he had given her a brotherly peck on the cheek.

So why had she spent her every waking hour thinking about Ryan Sheppard, when she had happily worked along-

side him for ages and always managed to keep him at a
healthy distance? Was she so emotionally stunted that she
had just switched infatuation? Did she have some kind of
insane inclination to fancy the men she worked for? *No!*
Jamie refused to concede any such thing. 'Because we have
a perfectly good working relationship and I don't want my
private life to start intruding on that.'

'Too bad. It already has.'

He abruptly leaned forward and Jamie automatically
pressed herself back into her chair.

'And,' he continued remorselessly, 'it's already affecting
your working life. That guy who appeared on your doorstep…'

'Greg,' Jamie conceded with reluctance. 'Jessica's husband.'

'Right. Greg. He's staying with you, is he?'

Jamie flushed and nodded. She looked wistfully at her
computer.

'And you have no objections to having your house turned
into a marriage counselling centre?'

'Of course I object to it! It's an absolute nightmare.'

'But they're still under your roof.'

'I don't see the point of discussing any of this.'

'The point is it's affecting your life and you can't separate the strands of your private life from your working life.
You look exhausted.'

'Thank you very much.'

'So what are you going to do about it?'

Jamie sighed with frustration and shot him a simmering, mutinous look from under her lashes. Ryan Sheppard
had a restless, curious mind. He could see things and approach them from different angles with a tenacity that always seemed to pay dividends. Where one person might
look at a failing company and walk away, he looked and then

looked a bit harder, and mentally began picking it apart until he could work out how to put it back together in a way that benefited him. Right now he was curious and, whilst she could hardly blame him, she had no intention of becoming his pet project.

But she grudgingly had to concede that he had a point when he said that the strands of her life were interwoven. She had shown up late for work because she had slept through her alarm, and she had slept through her alarm because Greg and Jessica had been engaged in one of their furious, long-winded arguments until the early hours of the morning. The muffled sound of their voices had wafted up the stairs and into her bedroom and she just hadn't been able to get to sleep.

Something in her stirred. She had never been a person to share her problems. Deep ingrained into her psyche was the notion that her problems belonged to her and no one else. It seemed suddenly tempting to offload a little.

'What *can* I do about it?' she muttered, fiddling with her pen.

'I can immediately think of one solution—kick them both out.'

'That's not an option. I'm not about to kick my sister out when she's come to me for help and support. Believe me, I know all of Jessica's failings. She can be childish and badly behaved and irresponsible, but in times of crisis she needs to know that she can turn to me.'

'She's a grown adult. She's fully capable of helping and supporting herself.' He was beating his head against a brick wall; he could see that. Lazily, he allowed his eyes to rove over her body, finally coming to rest of that full, downturned mouth. Out of the blue, he felt himself begin to harden and he abruptly looked away. Good God. It was as though his body was suddenly possessed of a mind of its own.

'You've met my sister. You can't really believe that.' Jamie smiled to lighten the mood, but Ryan's eyes remained grimly serious on her.

'Because you took her on as your responsibility at a young age doesn't mean that you're condemned to stick to the program till the day you die, Jamie.'

'My mother made me promise that I'd be there for her. I… You don't understand. I think of my mother asking me to make sure that I looked after Jessica, and my hands are tied. I couldn't let her down. And I couldn't let Greg down.'

Ryan stared at her and noticed the way she glanced away from him, offering him her delicate profile, noticed the way her skin coloured.

He thought back to that kiss, the way she had pulled him towards her and curved her small, supple body against his, offering her lips to him. And then Greg's appearance at the door, like an apparition stepping out of the wintry depths. His brain was mentally doing the maths.

'Why would that be?' he asked casually. Her eyes weren't on him as he strolled towards the coffee machine, which was just one of the many appliances he kept in his vast office to make life a bit easier when he was working through the night. He handed her a mug of coffee and Jamie absent-mindedly took it. It was her first cup of coffee of the morning and it tasted delicious.

'It's pretty hard on him,' she confessed, watching as Ryan rolled his chair towards her and took up position uncomfortably close. In fact, their knees were almost touching.

'Explain.'

'He's doing his best with my sister. She isn't the easiest person in the world. He's very calm and gentle but she more than makes up for it.'

'Calm and gentle,' Ryan mused thoughtfully.

'He's a vet. He has to be.'

'You worked for him, didn't you?'

Jamie shrugged and said defensively, 'I did, a million years ago. The point is, he likes talking to me. I think it helps.'

'He likes talking to you because you're a trained marriage counsellor?' Ryan found himself stiffening with instant dislike for the man. He had known types like him—the kind, caring, calm, gentle types who thought nothing of taking advantage of any poor sap with a tendency to mother.

'No, Ryan. I'm not a *trained marriage counsellor*, but I listen to what he says and I try to be constructive.'

'And yet you haven't constructively told the pair of them to clear off because they're wrecking your life. My guess is that your mother wouldn't like to think that you're sacrificing the quality of your life for the sake of your sister.'

'Not all of us are selfish!'

'I'd call it practical. Why did you leave?'

'I beg your pardon?'

'Why did you leave your job working for the gentle vet?'

'Oh.' Jamie could feel herself going bright red as she fished around for a suitable reply.

'Was it the weather?' Ryan asked helpfully as he drew his own conclusions.

'I... Um, I guess the weather did have something to do with my decision. And also...' Coherent thought returned to her at long last. 'Jessica was old enough to stand on her own two feet and I thought it was a good time to start exploring pastures new, so to speak...'

'And, I guess, with your sister marrying the caring, sharing vet.'

'Yes. There was someone to look after her.'

'But I suppose you must have built up some sort of empathetic relationship with our knight in shining armour who rescued you from your sister,' Ryan encouraged speculatively. His eyes were sharp and focused, noting every change of expression on her face. She had a remarkably expressive face. He wondered how he could ever have missed that, but then again this was new territory for both of them.

'Could you please stop being derogatory about Greg?'

Ryan glanced down. There was no need for him to ask her why. He already knew. Had she actually been in love with the guy? Of course she had. It was written all over her face. And that, naturally, would have been why she had fled the scene of the crime, so to speak. Had they slept together?

Ryan found that that was a thought he didn't like, not at all. Nor did he care for the fact that his conclusions were leading him inexorably in one direction.

That kiss she had given him, the kiss that had been playing on his mind for the past two days, had had its roots in something a lot more unsavoury than just a woman with a little too much wine in her system behaving out of character for the first time in her life.

She had seen Greg, and Greg had seen her, and she had succumbed to the oldest need in the world. The need to make another man jealous.

Had she been reminding Mr Vet of what he had missed? The sour taste of being used rose in Ryan's throat. It was a sensation he had never experienced. She had wanted to bury the incident between them. As far as he was concerned, he would fetch the shovels and help her.

'He doesn't have anyone else to talk to,' Jamie was saying now. 'He's an only child and I don't think his parents really ever approved of the marriage. At least, not from what Jessica's told me over the years. So he can't go to them for advice, and I suppose I'm the obvious choice to confide in because she's my sister and I know her.'

'And what pearls of wisdom have you thrown his way?' Ryan couldn't help the heavy sarcasm in his voice but Jamie barely seemed to notice. She was, he thought, too wrapped up in thoughts of her erstwhile lover.

She might complain about her house being invaded but chances were that she was loving every second of it.

'I've told him that he's just got to persevere.' She smiled drily. 'Who else is going to take Jessica off my hands?'

'Who else indeed?' Ryan murmured. 'So there's no end to this in sight?'

'Not at the moment. Not unless I change the locks on the front door.' Making light of the situation was about the only way Jamie felt she could deal with it, but her smile was strained. 'Things will sort themselves out when Christmas is done and dusted. I mean, Greg will have to return to work. He said that he's got cover at the moment but I think his animals will start missing him!'

Ryan stood up and began prowling through the office. Usually as easy-going and as liberal minded as the next man, he was outraged at the nagging, persistent notion that he had been manipulated to make another man jealous. He was also infuriatingly niggled at the thought that Jamie might have slept with the vet. Naturally, people were entitled to live their lives the way they saw fit, but nevertheless...

Could he have been that mistaken about her?

'And what if things don't sort themselves out over Christmas?'

'I prefer to be optimistic.'

'Maybe,' Ryan said slowly, 'what they both need is time on their own.'

'Do you think I haven't suggested that?' Jamie asked him sharply. 'Jessica has dug her heels in. She doesn't want to return to Scotland and Greg doesn't want to leave without her.'

'Wise man.' Ryan's voice was shrewd. 'She's an unexploded time bomb.'

'I don't see how this is helping anything,' Jamie inserted briskly. 'Course it's nice to talk, and thank you very much for listening, but…'

'Maybe they need time on their own away from Scotland. Being in the home environment might just pollute the situation.' He had absolutely zero knowledge when it came to psychoanalysis but he was more than happy to make it up as he went along.

A plan of action was coming to him and he liked it. More to the point, it was a plan that would benefit them both. He sat on the edge of his desk and looked at her.

'Pollute the situation?'

'You know what I'm getting at.'

'Where else are they going to go? I can't think that Greg has enough money to move them into a hotel indefinitely. Besides, that would only make things worse, being cooped up in a room twenty-four-seven. There would be a double homicide. Actually, it wouldn't get that far. Jessica would refuse to go along with the plan.'

Ryan made an indistinct but sympathetic noise and gave her time to consider the horror of housing a bickering couple for the indefinite future, because the caring vet might just prioritise his marriage over the animals pining for him in his absence.

'What a hellish prospect for you.' He egged the mixture as he scooted his chair back to his desk. 'I'll bet your sister doesn't exercise a lot of restraint when it comes to airing her opinions either.'

'That's why I was late,' Jamie glumly confessed. 'They were arguing into the early hours of the morning and I could hear them from my bedroom so I couldn't fall asleep. I was so tired this morning that I slept through the alarm.'

'I'm going to be joining my family in the Caribbean day

after tomorrow. Stunning house in the Bahamas, if I say so myself,' he murmured and Jamie nodded.

'Yes. I know—I booked the tickets, remember? Lucky you. I know what I should be covering while you're away but there are a couple of things you'll need to look at before you go. I'll make sure that I bring them in for you by the end of the day. Also, if your visit over runs, shall I get Graham to chair the shareholders' meeting on the eighth?'

Ryan had no intention of becoming bogged down in point-less detail. He frowned pensively up at the ceiling, his hands linked behind his head, then startled her by sitting forward suddenly and placing his hands squarely on his desk.

'Just an idea, but I think you should accompany me on my trip.'

For a few seconds Jamie wasn't sure that she had heard him correctly. Her mind was still half taken up with the technicalities of rearranging his schedule should he remain out of the country for longer than anticipated. There were a number of prickly clients who liked to deal with Ryan and Ryan alone, as the mover and shaker of the company. They would have to be coaxed into a replacement.

'Jamie!' Like a magician summoning someone out of a trance, Ryan snapped his fingers and she started and sur-faced to slowly consider the suggestion he had posed.

'Accompany you?' she repeated in confusion.

'Why not? From where I'm sitting it sure beats the hell out of having to duck for cover from verbal missiles in your own house.' He stood up, began pacing through his office. He peered down at the stack of papers he had inadvertently sent flying to the ground earlier, decided to tidy it all up later and stepped over them to make his way to his coffee machine so that he could help himself to another mug of coffee.

'Also,' he offered, 'your sister and the vet might benefit from not having you around. I know you probably feel obliged to offer free advice, but sometimes the last thing people need in a time of crisis is a do-gooder trying to sort things out on their behalf.'

'I am not a *do-gooder* trying to sort anything out!' Jamie denied heatedly and Ryan shrugged.

'Okay, maybe the vet would be better off fighting his own battles without relying on his trusty ex-assistant to join in the fray.'

Looked at from every angle, that was an insulting observation, but before Jamie could splutter into more heated defence he was continuing in a thoughtful voice,

'And if they both prefer to hang out their dirty laundry in neutral territory, and a hotel room is out of the equation, then your place is as good as any—without you in it. You'd be doing them a favour and you'd be doing yourself a favour. No more sleepless nights. No more war zones to be avoided. No more playing piggy-in-the-middle. Chances are that by the time you get back they will have resolved their differences and cleared off and your life can return to normal.'

The promise of normality dangled in front of Jamie's eyes like a pot of gold at the end of a rainbow. She was in danger of forgetting what it was like.

'I couldn't possibly intrude on your family holiday.' She turned him down politely. 'But,' she said slowly, 'it *might* be a good idea if I weren't around. Perhaps—and I know this is very last-minute—I could book a few days' holiday?'

'Out of the question.' Ryan swallowed a mouthful of coffee and eyed her over the rim of the mug.

'But if I can leave here to go to the Caribbean, then surely I could leave to go somewhere else?' The weather was immaterial. It was the prospect of putting distance between Jessica, Greg and herself that was so tantalising. The Far East sounded just about right, never mind the jet lag.

'You can come to the Caribbean because I could use you over there. As you know, I'm combining my holiday with the business trip to Florida to give that series of presentations on trying to get our computer technology into greener cars.'

He glanced at the papers lying on the ground and strolled over to roughly gather them up and dump them on his desk. 'Still, sadly, in a state of semi-preparation.' He indicated the papers with a sweeping gesture while Jamie looked at him, unconvinced. Ryan rarely gave speeches that were fully prepared. He was clever enough and confident enough to earn a standing ovation by simply thinking on his feet. His grasp of the minutest details to do with the very latest cutting-edge technology was legendary.

'You could consider it something of a working holiday. I could get up to speed with these presentations before I fly to Florida. And,' he added for good measure, 'it's not as though you haven't travelled with me on business before...'

Which was a very valid reason for having her there—business. Of course, he was the first to acknowledge that it wasn't *exactly* the only reason for having her there. He genuinely thought that her presence in the house with her warring, uninvited guests was doing her no good whatsoever and there was also the small question of his curiosity; that was a little less easy to justify. But those recent revealing glimpses of her had roused his interest; why not combine his concern for her welfare with his semi-pressing need to get his presentations done and wrap them both up in a neat solution? Made sense.

He uneasily registered that there was a third reason. His mother and his sisters were relentlessly concerned with his moral welfare. His sisters had an annoying habit of bustling around him, trying to impose their opinions, and his mother specialised in meaningful chats about people who worked too hard.

Jamie would be a very useful buffer. There would be considerably less chance of being cornered if he made sure that she was floating somewhere in the vicinity whenever the going looked as though it might get dicey. Were he to be on his own, any attempt to excuse himself on the pretext of having to work would be thoroughly disregarded. With Jamie around, however, even his sisters would reluctantly be forced to keep a low profile in the name of simple courtesy.

'It's not the same.'

'Huh? What's not the same?'

'You're going to be with your family,' Jamie said patiently. 'Doing family stuff.' She wasn't entirely sure what that entailed. Family stuff, for her, had long meant stretches of tension and uncomfortable confrontations simmering just below the surface.

'Oh, they will already have done the family stuff over their turkey on Christmas day. They'll be desperate to see a new face and my mother won't stop thanking you for showing up. When my sisters get together, they revert to childhood. They giggle and swap clothes and waste hours applying make-up on each other while their men take over babysitting duties and countdown to when they can start on the rum cocktails. My mother says that it's impossible to get a serious word out of them when they're together. She'll love you.'

'Because I'm serious and boring?'

'Serious? Boring?' His dark eyes lingered on her and Jamie flushed and looked away. 'Hardly. In fact, having seen you over—'

'Who would cover for me in my absence?' she interrupted hastily just in case he decided to travel down

Memory Lane and dredge up her un-secretary-like behaviour on Christmas day.

Ryan dismissed that concern with a casual wave of his hand before giving her a satisfied smile.

'I haven't agreed to anything,' Jamie informed him. 'If you really think that you might need me there to help with the presentations...'

'Absolutely. You would be vital. You know I can't manage without you.'

'I don't want you to think that I'm in need of rescuing.' Sometimes that dark, velvety voice literally sent a shiver through her, even though she knew that it was in his nature to flirt. 'I don't. I might be in an awkward position just at the moment, but it's nothing that I wouldn't be able to handle.'

'I don't doubt that for a second,' Ryan dutifully agreed. 'You'd be doing *me* a favour.'

'Won't your family think it a bit strange for you to be dragging a perfect stranger along to their family celebrations?'

'Nothing fazes my family, believe me. Besides, what's one more to the tally?' He lowered his eyes. 'You have no excuse for refusing unless, of course, you can't bear to lose your role of personal adviser to the vet.'

'His name is Greg.' It was weird but Greg's effect on her was not what she had expected. She had always imagined that seeing him again would catapult her back to that time when she had been firmly in his power and used to weave innocent fantasies about him. She always thought that she would be reduced to blushing, stammering and possibly making a fool of herself but she hadn't. His allure had disappeared over the years. Now she just felt sorry for him and the situation in which her sister had placed him.

Watching her, Ryan felt a spurt of irritation that she had ignored the better part of his remark.

'Well?' he prodded. 'Do you think that you're too invaluable as unpaid counsellor to take a few days away from them? We'll be there for roughly five days. My sisters and their various other halves and children will leave at the beginning of the New Year. We will stay for a further three days until my conferences are due to begin and you can fly back to London when I fly to Florida. It's a lot to pass on, for the sake of being the vet's sounding board. Are you worried that he might not be able to survive this crisis without your input?'

'Of course I'm not!'

'Then why the hesitation?'

'I told you, I don't want to intrude.'

'And *I* told *you* you won't be intruding.'

'And I don't,' she belatedly pointed out, 'think that I'm invaluable to Greg. Like I said, I'm the only one he feels comfortable discussing all of this with.' Once upon a time, she might have been flattered, but now she was just impatient. 'But you're right—you're my boss. If I'm needed in a work capacity, then I'm more than happy to oblige. I'm very committed to my job, as you know.'

'I'm not a slave driver, Jamie. I won't be standing over you wielding a whip and making sure that I get my money's worth. Yes, we will do some work, but you'll have ample time to relax and de-stress. It'll be worth it to have you back in one piece when we resume work in January.'

Jamie nodded briskly. Whichever way it was wrapped up, Ryan was doing this for his own benefit. She had been inconsistent recently and he didn't like that. She was his efficient, well-run, well-oiled secretary and that was what he wanted back. It was why she was paid so handsomely. He could easily do whatever work he needed to do without her, but he had decided that her home life was interfering with her work life and, since her work life was the only thing that mattered to him, he was prepared to take her with him, away from the chaotic environment in which she now found herself.

'I'll see to the ticket, shall I?'

'First-class, with me. And sort out your replacement for while you're away. It's a quiet time. There shouldn't be anything that can't be handled by someone else for a short while.'

'Is there anything in particular you'd like me to read up on before we get out there? I wouldn't want to come unprepared.'

Ryan narrowed his eyes but her face was bland, helpful and utterly unreadable.

But that, he thought with a kick of satisfaction, was just an illusion, wasn't it? Strip away the mask and she was a hotbed of undiscovered fire.

'Nope. No reading to be done. But you might want to think about packing a few swimsuits. I'm going to insist that you enjoy yourself, like a good boss, and the house comes with an amazing pool. And don't look so appalled. When this is over, you're going to thank me.'

CHAPTER FIVE

So far she *had* thanked him; on at least four separate occasions she had thanked him. She had thanked him variously for giving her the opportunity to enjoy 'such a wonderful place', for allowing her to relax in 'such amazing surroundings', it was a 'guilty pleasure'. She had thanked him the day before when he had shooed her off to explore the tiny nearby town with his sisters. She had thanked him when he had insisted that there was no need for her to wake at the crack of dawn with her laptop at the ready, just because he happened to need very little sleep and enjoyed working first thing in the mornings.

Her copious gratitude was getting on his nerves. He had been hoping to reacquaint himself with the intriguing new face he had glimpsed behind her polite, efficient mask but so far nothing. Although, to be fair, his plans for her to be a buffer between himself and any awkward conversations with his family members had been spectacularly successful and he was rarely in her company without some member of the troupe tagging along, unless they were specifically working.

They had established one of the downstairs rooms as a makeshift office but its air-conditioned splendour, whilst practical, felt sterile when through the windows they could see the stretching gardens, fragrant and colourful with tropical flowers which spilled their vibrancy under the palm trees. So they had migrated to one of the many shady areas of the wide veranda that circled the house. Which, in turn, meant that they were open to interruption, sometimes from one of the four kids belonging to two of his sisters who used outside as their playground. Sometimes from one of his sisters or—and he would have to fling his arms up and concede defeat when this happened—all three. And sometimes from his mother, who would appear with a tray of cold drinks and proceed to embark on a meandering conversation with Jamie to whom she seemed to have taken a keen liking. This was partly because Jamie was such a good listener and partly because his mother was, by nature, a sociable woman.

But when they were alone together, Jamie was not to be distracted from what she considered the primary purpose of her all-expenses-paid winter break. The very second they were together, their conversation focused entirely on work and on progressing a series of elaborate flip charts in which Ryan had no interest and probably wouldn't use anyway. She asked him innumerable questions about various technicalities to do with car manufacture, displaying an admirable breadth of knowledge, but, the minute he attempted to manoeuvre the conversation to something a little more interesting and a little more personal, she smiled, clammed up and he was obliged to return to the subject in hand.

Right now, the evening meal was finished. Two of his sisters were settling their children, who ranged in ages from three to six. They would be chivvying their husbands, Tom and Patrick, into performing a variety of duties and neither would be released until those duties were satisfactorily completed. His sisters were nothing if not bossy. Susie—older than him by two years, and seven months pregnant—had disappeared back to England with her husband. The house was at least becoming quieter. It would be quieter still in a day's time when his other sisters headed back to their various homes.

Enjoying the peace of the gardens and lost in his thoughts, Ryan was only aware of Jamie's presence nearby by the low murmur of her voice.

His ears instantly pricked up. He had assumed that she had retreated to the conservatory with a cup of coffee.

Naturally, he knew that it was beyond rude not to announce his presence by making some obvious noise—rustling a few leaves or launching into a coughing fit, perhaps.

Instead, he endeavoured to make as little noise as possible. Of course, if she looked around carefully, she would be able to spot him, although it was dark and this part of the extensive gardens was a lattice-work of trees and shrubbery leading to the infinity pool, which overlooked the sea from the cliff on which the house was majestically perched.

The breeze was warm and salty and ruffled the fronds of the palm trees, leaves and flowers like a very gentle caress. In the distance the sea stretched, flat and black, towards the horizon.

And down the small flight of stone steps Ryan spotted her, sitting by the pool in darkness, talking softly into her mobile phone.

If she needed to make a call, she could have used the landline; he had told her this at the very start. Instead, she had chosen to sneak off to the pool so that she could...*what*? Conduct a clandestine conversation? And with whom? The vet, of course.

His lips thinned and he sprinted down the steps, appearing in front of her so suddenly that she gave a little shriek and dropped the phone.

'Oh, dear. Did I startle you?' He bent to retrieve the mobile which lay in various pieces on the ground.

Jamie, half standing, scrabbled to get the phone from

him as he clicked various bits back together, put it to his ear, shook it and then shrugged. 'You got cut off. Sorry. And I think the phone might be broken.'

'What are you doing here?' Over the past three days she had contrived not to be alone in his presence at all. Away from the safety net of the office, she had felt vulnerable and threatened in this island paradise. There was just too much of him for her liking. Too much of him wearing shorts, going barefoot, bare chested, getting slowly bronzed. Too much of him lazing around, teasing his sisters, letting them boss him around and then rolling his eyes heavenwards so that one of them laughed and playfully smacked him. Too much of him being silly with the children who clearly adored him. Too much of him being a *man* instead of being her boss. It unnerved her.

'What are *you* doing here?' He threw the question back at her, then sat down on one of the wooden deck chairs and patted the one next to him so that she reluctantly joined him. 'If you needed to make a call, you know that you could have used the landline. I did tell you that.'

'Yes, well…' She could barely make him out. He was all shadows and angles, and rakish in his low-slung khaki shorts and an old tee-shirt. To see him, no one would have guessed that he was a multi-millionaire.

'Personal call, was it?' Ryan prompted, undeterred by her reluctance to talk. 'How are they back home? Still alive and kicking, or has you sister put the vet out of his misery? I'm thinking that if they had sorted out their differences and returned to Scotland in the throes of rekindled love you would have reported it back to me.'

The darkness enfolding them in its embrace lent an air of intimacy that Jamie found disturbing. In fact, her heart was beating like a hammer inside her and her mouth felt horribly, treacherously dry. She physically longed for it to

be daylight, with Claire, Hannah and Susie lurking nearby,
and a flip chart behind which she could conveniently hide.

'Nothing's been sorted as yet,' Jamie conceded grudgingly. She felt very visible in her shorts and small striped
vest, but it had been the first thing to hand after she had had
a shower half an hour earlier. She hadn't expected to run
into Ryan lurking like an intruder in the shadows.

'Oh, dear,' Ryan murmured sympathetically. 'Was that
the vet on the phone?'

'Will you *please* stop calling him the vet?'

'Sorry, but I thought that's what he did for a living—
tended to all those wounded animals who pined for him in
his absence.'

Jamie glanced across at him but he was a picture of in-
nocence. The light breeze ruffled his hair and he looked
perfectly relaxed, a man at home in his surroundings.

'Yes, it was Greg, as a matter of fact.'

'Making a secretive call behind his wife's back? Hmm...'

'It wasn't a secretive call!'

'Then what was it? Obviously not a call you felt comfortable taking in front of the family.'

'You're impossible!'

'So what did the vet have to say?'

Jamie gritted her teeth together. Ryan was provocative by
nature; it was nothing personal. They had both also strayed
so far from their boundaries that the lines between them
were getting blurred. She had met his family, seen him relaxed in his own home territory. She, in turn, had confided
things she wouldn't have dreamt possible. But he was accustomed to breaking down boundaries and getting into the
heads of other people; it was part and parcel of what made
him a success. And if *she* found it impossible to deal with
then it was a reflection on her, and to start huffing and puff-
ing now and trying to evade his natural curiosity would seem

strange. Strange was the one thing she knew was dangerous. It was an instinctive realisation. So what was the big deal in telling him what was going on with Greg and Jessica? It wasn't as though he was out of the loop. He was firmly embedded in it, thanks to a sequence of circumstances which she might not have invited but which had happened nevertheless.

'Jessica told me that the reason she felt that she needed more space was because she felt bored and isolated where they live. It's at least forty minutes into Edinburgh, and Jessica has always liked to be in the thick of things.'

'Odd match, in that case.'

'What do you mean?'

'I mean that the vet didn't strike me as the sort of man who prides himself on having a wild social life. I can't see him being the life and soul of any party.'

'You met him for five minutes! You don't know him at all.'

'Oh, yes, I'm forgetting that you two shared a special bond.'

'We didn't share a *special bond*.' But she could feel herself flushing, thinking about her youthful, romantic dreams.

Ryan ignored her heated protest. He didn't have to see her face to be able to take stock of the fact that she was flustered by what he had said—but then she would be, he thought edgily. He was beginning to loathe the caring vet with his menagerie of loyal animals.

'So what did your flamboyant sister see in him?' he persisted.

'He's absolutely one-hundred-percent devoted to her.'

'Ah, but is it mutual? One-way devotion could become trying after a while, I should imagine.'

'Won't your family be wondering where we are?'

'We're adults. I don't suppose they'll be worried in case

we miss our footing and fall in the pool by accident. Besides, Claire and Hannah are doing their nightly battle with the children, and my mother was feeling tired and took herself off to bed with a book and a cup of hot chocolate. So you can put that concern of yours to rest!'

'You have a fantastic family.' Jamie sighed wistfully, and for a moment Ryan was sufficiently distracted to silently wait until she expanded. Women always enjoyed talking about themselves. In fact, from his experience, they would hold court until the break of dawn given half a chance, but generally speaking their conversations were usually targeted to sexually attract. They flirted and pouted and always portrayed themselves in the best possible light. In the case of the women he dated—supermodels and actresses—their anecdotes were usually fond recollections of their achievements on stage or on the runway, often involving getting the better of their competition.

'A bit different from yours, I expect,' he murmured encouragingly when his lengthy silence didn't appear to be working.

'Totally different. You never talk about them.'

'And you've only now started talking about yours.'

'Yes, well, my situation is nothing like yours. When I think of Jessica, I start getting stressed. But *your* sisters… they're very easy-going.'

Ryan grinned. 'I have vague recollections of the three of them trying out their make-up on me when I was younger. Not so easy-going for me, I can tell you.'

Jamie laughed. She couldn't help herself.

'Still, it was tougher on you, raising a teenager when you weren't even out of your teens yourself.'

Lost in her thoughts, she was seduced by the warm interest in his voice, by the soft, warm breeze and the gentle, rhythmic sound of waves breaking against the cliff face.

She felt inclined to share, especially after her conversation with Greg.

'Even before Mum died, Jessica was a handful. I just did my own thing, but she was always demanding, even as a child. She was just so beautiful and she could twist Mum round her little finger. When I look at your sisters and see the way they share everything... Anyway.' She pulled herself together. 'I always think that there's no point weeping and wailing over stuff you can't change.'

'Quite. You were telling me about your conversation with the vet. You thought that your sister was bored because she was a party animal and the vet only enjoyed the company of his sick animals.'

'I never said any such thing!'

'I'm reading between the lines. Have you got an update on the real situation?'

Of course, Jamie thought, brought down to earth, he was keen to find out whether matters were being sorted. He needed her back and functioning in one piece, and the sooner Greg and Jessica sorted themselves out and cleared off the better for him. She would do well to remind herself that his interest was mostly self-motivated. She would also do well to realise that allowing herself to slip into a state of familiarity with him just because he happened to know a little bit more about her private life than he ever had would be madness. There was no chance that she could ever be interested in him in the way that she had been interested in Greg, because Greg represented just the sort of gentle, caring person she found attractive. But still...

'I think we might be seeing the true cause of everything that's been happening between Greg and my sister,' she told him crisply. 'Apparently Greg wants children and he thinks that it's a good time for them to start trying. That seems to have caused everything to explode.'

'Your sister isn't interested?'

'She hasn't mentioned a word of it to me,' Jamie said with a shrug. 'I'm guessing that she might have been feeling a bit bored, but the minute Greg mentioned kids she took fright and started feeling trapped. The only thing she could think of doing was to escape, hence her appearance on my doorstep. At least there's something tangible now to deal with, so you can relax. I'm sure they'll both get to the bottom of their problems by the time I return to England, and once they've disappeared back to Scotland everything will return to normal. I won't be arriving late to work and I'll be as focused as I've always been.'

She stood up and brushed the backs of her thighs where tiny specks of sand had stuck from the chair. She did her best to ignore his dark eyes thoughtfully watching her.

'So what are our plans for tomorrow? I know that your sisters leave with Tom and Patrick and the kids. I have no objection to working in the evening. You've been more than kind in letting me take so much time off to relax.'

'Let's not get back on that gratitude bandwagon,' Ryan said irritably. His eyes skimmed over her, taking in her slender legs, slim waist and pert breasts barely contained underneath the vest. Her work suits did nothing to flatter her figure. The memory of her full mouth pressed against his flashed through his head and ignited a series of images that made him catch his breath sharply. 'I haven't seen you at the pool,' he continued, standing up and swamping her with his potently masculine presence. Jamie instinctively took a small step backwards.

'I... I've sat there with my book a bit.'

'But not been tempted to get in the water. Don't you swim?'

'Yes.' She *had* stuck on her black bikini on one occasion, but the thought of parading in a pool in a bikini with

Ryan—her boss—splashing around, having fun with the family, had been too much. She had promptly taken it off and replaced it with her summer shift. Much safer.

'Then why the reticence? Did you feel shy with my noisy family all around?'

'No. Of course not!'

'Well, they'll be gone by tomorrow evening, and things will be a lot quieter here. You can start enjoying the pool in peace and quiet.'

'Maybe. I really should be getting in now.'

'Wild imagination here, but I get the feeling you don't like being alone with me. A guy could get offended.'

Jamie tensed. His lazy teasing was dangerously unsettling.

'Correct me if I'm wrong, but I spent three hours alone with you today.'

'Ah, but in the company of a flip chart, two computers and a range of stationery.'

'I'm just doing my job! It's what I'm paid to do and I'm going to head back now.'

Up the stone steps leading down to the pool, the path skirted the house, taking them across the sprawling gardens where palm trees fringed the edges, leaning towards the sea. Underneath, a huge variety of plants and shrubs were landscaped to provide a wild, untamed feel to the garden.

Jamie's feet seemed to have wings. She was acutely conscious of Ryan behind her. She had never been very self-confident about her body. With Jessica as a sister, she had been too aware growing up of the physical differences between them. She was shorter, her figure so much less eye-catching. And she was wearing shorts!

Of their own accord, her thoughts flew back to the parade of models who had flitted in and out of Ryan's life: blondes with legs to their armpits and hair to their waists.

Unconscious comparisons sprang to mind, addling her, and maybe that was why she stumbled over the root of a tree projecting above-ground, walking so quickly, rigid as a plank of wood, arms protectively folded and her mind all over the place. It was a recipe for disaster on a dark night in unfamiliar surroundings.

She gave a soft gasp as her body made painful contact with the ground but before she could stagger to her feet she was being lifted up as though she weighed nothing.

Jamie shrieked. 'Put me down! What are you doing?'

'Calm down.'

The feel of his muscular arms around her and the touch of his hard chest set up a series of tingling reactions in her body that made her writhe in his arms until she realised that her writhing was having just the opposite effect; he tightened his hold, pulling her more firmly against him. Instantly, she fell limp and allowed herself to be carried up to the veranda where he gently deposited her on one of the wicker chairs which were strewn at various intervals around the house.

'I'm absolutely fine,' she muttered through gritted teeth and was ignored as Ryan stooped down and removed her espadrilles.

His long fingers gently felt her foot and her ankle, which he ordered her to try and move.

'I haven't twisted anything!' she exclaimed, trying to pull her foot out of his grasp while her treacherous body was tempted to go with the flow and succumb to the wonderful sensation of what his hands were doing.

'No. If you had, you wouldn't be able to move it.'

'Exactly. So if you don't mind...'

'But you're bruised.' He was peering at her knee and then doing it again, sweeping her up and informing her that it was just as well to put no strain on it but that she needed cleaning up.

'That's something I can do myself.' Her breasts were pushing against his chest and, good lord, her nipples were hardening as they scraped against the fabric of her bra, and between her legs felt damp. Every bit of her body was responding to him and she hated it. It terrified the life out of her. She just wanted him to put her down so that she could scuttle back to the safety of her bedroom, but instead he was carrying her through the house, up the short staircase that led to the wing of the house where he was staying and then—when it couldn't get any worse as far as she was concerned—into his bedroom. Jamie closed her eyes and stifled a weak groan of despair.

She hadn't been here yet. His room was huge and dominated by an impressive bed fashioned out of bamboo. The linen was a colourful medley of bold reds and blacks and looked positively threatening.

Beneath the window was a long sofa and he took her to it and sat her down.

'Don't move a muscle. I have a first-aid kit in the bathroom—hangover from my Boy Scout days.'

'This is ridiculous—and you were never a Boy Scout!'

'Of course I was!' He disappeared into the adjoining bathroom and through the open door Jamie glimpsed him rifling through a cupboard, searching out the first-aid kit. 'I may even have earned a few badges.' He reappeared with a small tin and knelt at her feet. 'If you ever need a tent erecting, or a fire to be lit using only two pieces of wood, then I'm your man. Tsk, tsk—do you see those bruises on your knees? If you hadn't been rushing off like a bat out of hell this would never have happened.'

Jamie clamped her teeth together and refrained from telling him that if he hadn't appeared in front of her, broken her phone and then insisted on having a long, personal conversation with her she wouldn't have felt inclined to rush off and wouldn't be sitting here now in his bedroom while he...

She squeezed her eyes tightly shut, intending to block out the image of his down-bent head as he tended to her bruises, applying alcohol wipes to the surfaces, then antiseptic cream which he gently rubbed into her skin.

'No good applying any plasters,' he informed her. 'You want the sun to dry out these cuts and scratches.'

'Yep, okay. Thank you. I'll leave now, if you don't mind.'

'Shall I carry you?'

Her eyes flew open and she saw that he was grinning at her.

'Don't be ridiculous!'

'And to continue our conversation...'

'To continue our conversation about *what*?'

'About tomorrow, of course.'

She caught his eyes. He looked as innocent as the pure driven snow.

'What about tomorrow?' she stammered, walking towards the door.

'Well, you were telling me about what you wanted to do. Work wise.'

Had she? She couldn't think. Every nerve ending in her body was on fire. She was tingling all over and it was ludicrous. Having an insane crush on Greg had been bad enough but at least she could see the sense there. With Ryan Sheppard? She didn't even respect the sort of guy who dated a string of models, who never seemed to see beyond the long legs and the perfect figure! Ergo, she couldn't possibly have a crush on him. The soaring tropical heat was getting to her. She wasn't used to it.

'Yes!' The place was going to be empty, aside from his mother. Suddenly, the thought of even a tiny window when they would be together without the possibility of interruption was scary beyond belief. 'There are still loads of things to do and I have lots of ideas about your presentations—like, you really need to give a strong argument for implementing your system in their cars. New technology can do so much for the environment.'

She had reached the door without even realizing. Now her back was against the door frame and he was looking at her with his head to one side, the picture-perfect image of someone one-hundred-percent interested in what she had to say.

So why the heck was she feeling so nervous?

She quailed when he took a few steps towards her.

'Are you entirely sure that you're all right?'

He loomed over her, a darkly, wickedly sexy guy who was sending her mind into crazy disarray.

'Because you've gone pale.' He leant against the door frame and looked at her with concern. 'Nothing broken, but you could still be in a bit of shock at losing your footing like that. Happens, you know—you have a minor accident and you think you're fine but really...'

'I don't *think* I'm fine. I *am* fine.'

'I think we can afford to give work a miss tomorrow. Those harridans known as my sisters will be leaving, and as soon as they've gone the house is going to feel very empty. It might be an idea to do something with my mother, occupy her...'

'I'm more than happy to do that.'

'I think I might like to be included in the exercise,' Ryan murmured drily, looking down at her. She noticed the fine lines around his eyes that spoke of a man who lived life to the full, the thick sweep of his dark lashes, the deep bitter-chocolate of his irises flecked with tinges of gold. He was beautiful but not in a detached, frozen way. He was beautiful in a devastatingly sexy way and her pulses raced in easy, treacherous recognition of that.

'Of course! Actually, I think it might be a good idea if you and your mother had some, um, time together. You've hardly had a one to one with her since we got here.'

'Oh, there's no need for a one to one. Can I let you in on a little secret?' he murmured huskily, leaning towards her.

Jamie nodded because quite honestly she didn't trust herself to speak. She didn't think her voice would sound normal because her tongue appeared to be glued to the roof of her mouth.

'One to ones with my mother can sometimes be a little dangerous.'

'What are you talking about?' Locked into this intimate atmosphere, she found it impossible to tear herself away from his mesmeric dark gaze.

'She's developed an unnerving habit of cornering me about my private life.' In actual fact, Ryan hadn't meant to mention this at all. Underneath the confident, self-assured charm he was a lot more watchful and contained than people suspected, but he wanted to get under her skin. With each passing day, the desire had grown more urgent. He was frustrated by the way she blocked him, and frustrated with himself for a curiosity he couldn't understand. On a basic level, he realised that the confidences she had shared with him—which would hardly be termed earth shattering by most people's standards—were hugely significant for her. Possibly she regretted them. Scratch that—she *did* regret them but she was now unable to retreat.

However, that didn't mean that she was now on a new, no-holds-barred, sharing level with him. And he wanted her there. He actively wanted her to invite him into her thoughts—which would entail some confidence sharing of his own.

So, when she looked at him in silent curiosity, he heard himself say with utmost seriousness, 'I'm not sure that my mother is a firm believer in the virtues of playing the field. Nor, for that matter, are the harridans.'

'I don't think that there's any mother who would be thrilled to have a son who takes the fastest exit the second there's the threat of commitment with a woman.'

'Is that what you think I do?'

'Isn't it?' The silence that greeted her question was thick and heavy with a peculiar, thrilling undercurrent. Jamie desperately wanted to repeat her mantra about going to bed, but a weird and powerful sense of anticipation held her to the spot. When after a few seconds he didn't answer, she shrugged lightly and began turning away.

'Well, it's none of my business anyway. Although I resent the fact that you feel it permissible to ask whatever questions you like about my private life, even though you know that I don't want to answer them, and yet you can't be bothered to answer any that are directed at you. Not,' she added for good measure, her hand on the door frame, 'that I care one way or another.'

'I could be hurt by that,' Ryan murmured softly. 'You're my irreplaceable secretary. You're supposed to care.' It wasn't his imagination; when it came to women, he had the instincts of a born predator. He knew when they were reacting to him and Jamie was reacting to him right now. It was there in the slight flare of her nostrils, the faint flush that spread across her cheeks and the way her pupils dilated. Her mouth was half-open, as though she was on the verge of saying something, and her full, parted lips allowed a glimpse of her pearl-white teeth.

The urge to press her against the door frame and kiss her senseless was as overpowering as a blow to the stomach. He wanted to slide his hand underneath that tiny vest of hers and feel the weight of her breast against the palm of his hand. He wanted to taste her, right here, right now on his bed.

Interest and curiosity were one thing, being torn apart by inexplicable sexual desire was another. Jamie Powell might have suddenly become dangerously intriguing but it would be lunacy to follow it through simply to see where it led. For a start, she was the best secretary he had ever had. For another, she was no bimbo ready and willing for a romp in the hay, no strings attached.

'You're right. It's none of your business.'

'Good night, Ryan. Thanks for taking care of my cuts and bruises.'

He reached out and his long fingers circled her arm. 'My father took his eye off the ball,' Ryan told her softly. 'He got married, had four children... Like I said, he took his eye off the ball. While he was busy being domesticated, his finance director was helping himself to company funds. By the time my father noticed, the company was virtually on its knees. In my view, he worked himself into an early grave trying to get it back in order but by then it was too late. I inherited a mess, and I got it where it should be, and I have no intention of taking my own eye off the ball. Thanks to my efforts, my mother has the lifestyle she deserves and my sisters have the financial security they deserve. So, you see, I have no time for the demands of a committed relationship. I don't need the distraction.'

Jamie found that she was holding her breath.

'So you're never going to get married? Have kids? Become a grandfather?'

'If I do, it will be on my terms to someone who is willing to take second place to the fact that my primary concern is being one-hundred-and-ten-percent hands-on with my company. There's nothing that goes on at RS Enterprises that I don't know about. That situation exists because I make sure that I never let my attention slip.'

'Lucky lady, whoever snaps you up,' Jamie murmured with sarcasm and Ryan released her and laughed softly and appreciatively.

'I date women who understand where I'm coming from.'

'Was Leanne the exception?'

'Leanne knew the score the minute she became involved with me. I'm honest to a fault.' He couldn't read a thing in the cool, brown eyes assessing him. He continued, irritated by what he took to be silent criticism from Jamie. 'I never make promises I can't fulfil and I never encourage a woman to think that she's got her feet in the door. I don't ask them to share my space. I discourage items of clothing from being left overnight at my apartment. I warn them that I'm unpredictable with my time.'

Jamie marvelled that he could still think that just because he laid down ground rules hearts would never be broken.

'Maybe you should tell your mother that.' Jamie snapped out of her trance and broke eye contact with him. 'Then perhaps she would stop cornering you with awkward questions.'

The shutters were back down. Ryan wondered whether he had imagined that response he had seen in her. Had he? Disconcerted, he frowned and half turned away.

'Maybe I'll do that.' He smiled at her with equal politeness. 'Honesty, after all, is always the best policy...'

CHAPTER SIX

CLAIRE and Hannah, their husbands and children left in a flurry of forgotten stuffed toys that needed to be fetched, a thousand things that had to be ticked off their check list and lots of hugs and kisses and promises to meet up just as soon as life returned to normal. And then they were gone and the house felt suddenly very quiet and very empty.

In two days' time, Ryan would take one plane to Florida while she took another back to England and Vivian, his mother, would stay on for a further week, joined by several of her friends for their annual bridge holiday.

With Vivian excusing herself for an afternoon nap and Ryan announcing that he intended to work, waving her down when she immediately started to talk about what they would be doing, Jamie found herself at a loose end. For the first time, she realised that it was a relief to have been deprived of her mobile phone. Normally, she would have been following the crisis between Greg and her sister in a state of barely suppressed stress, but without the means of contacting them unless she used the landline, which she didn't intend to, she felt guiltily liberated from the problem—at least temporarily.

For the first time since she had arrived, she decided to take advantage of the empty swimming pool, and was there in her bikini with her towel, her sun block and a book within forty minutes.

It felt like a holiday. The pool offered spectacular views of the sea and was surrounded by palm trees and foliage, ripe with butterflies and the sound of birds. Jamie lay down on her sun lounger and let her mind wander, and every one of its meanderings returned to Ryan. His image seemed to have been stamped on her brain and she wasn't sure whether that had always been the case or whether it was something that had occurred ever since some of the barriers between them had been eroded. Had she been sucked into his charming, witty, intelligent personality without even realising? Or had all that charm, wit and intelligence only begun working on her once he had uncovered some of those private details that she had striven so hard to keep from him?

She had been determined never to repeat the folly of getting personally involved with the boss. Falling for Greg had been a youthful indiscretion and she could now look back on that younger self with a certain amount of wry amusement, because her crush had been so *harmless*.

This situation with Ryan was altogether more dangerous because Ryan was just a more dangerous man. There were times when she physically reacted to him with something that was unconscious and almost primitive in its intensity, and when she thought about that she wanted to close her eyes and faint with the horror of it.

In comparison, her silly infatuation with Greg was exposed for what it had really been: something harmless that had occurred at just the time she had needed it. An innocent distraction from the stress and trauma of her home life. She had taken refuge in her pleasant daydreams, and her working life, which had involved spending hours in Greg's company, had been a soothing panacea against the harsh reality that had been waiting to greet her the second she had walked back through the front door at the end of the evening.

Greg had been kind, thoughtful and gentle and he had been a buffer between herself and the disappointment of having to give up on her dreams of going to university.

Ryan, however...

Yes, he was kind and thoughtful and gentle. She had seen it in a thousand ways in his interaction with his sisters, his mother, his nephews and nieces. But he was no Greg. There was a core of steel running through him that made her shiver with a kind of dangerous excitement that enthralled and scared her at the same time. When his dark eyes rested on her, she didn't feel a pleasurable flutter, she felt a wild rush of adrenalin that left her breathless and exposed.

It would be a relief to return to England. She hoped that Greg and Jessica would have sorted out their differences by then, but even if they hadn't she would still be returning to the protection of the office, her colleagues and the self-imposed distance between boss and secretary. Out here, a million miles away from her home territory, it was too easy for the lines between them to be eroded.

She flipped over onto her stomach, but even after half an hour, and with her sun protection liberally applied, Jamie was beginning to feel burnt. The sun out here was like nothing she had felt before. It was fierce and unrelenting, especially at this hour of the day. When she tried to read her book, her eyes felt tired from the white glare and after a while she dragged the wooden lounger under the partial shade afforded by an overhanging tree.

Then, when she began feeling uncomfortable even in the shade, she dived into the pool. Pure bliss: the water was like cool silk around her. She began swimming, revisiting a pleasurable activity which she had indulged only occasionally in London, because her working hours were long and she just never seemed to find the time.

Like a fish, she ducked below the surface of the water, mentally challenging herself to swim the length of the pool without surfacing for air.

Uncomfortable thoughts began to gel in her head as she swam, reaching one end, gulping in air and then setting off again.

She had given up going to the swimming baths because of her work. She had given up going to the gym three times a week because of her work. She made arrangements to see friends in the evening but had often cancelled at a moment's notice because Ryan had needed her to do overtime. She had thought nothing of it.

She had assumed herself to be a goal-focused person. She had patted herself on the back for being someone who was prepared to go the distance because she was ambitious and worth every penny of the three pay rises she had been given in the space of eighteen months. She had never thought that maybe she had gone that extra mile because she had enjoyed the opportunity of being with Ryan. Had she been the ever-obliging secretary because, without even realising it, she had wanted to feed a secret craving? Had she been smugly pleased with herself for having learnt a lesson from her experience with Greg, only to be ambushed by repeating her mistake without even realising it?

That thought was so disturbing that she was unaware of the wall of the pool rushing towards her as she skimmed underneath the water. She bumped her head and was instantly shocked into spluttering up to the surface.

When she opened her eyes, blinking the water out of them, it was to find Ryan leaning over the side of the pool like a vision conjured up from her feverish imagination, larger than life.

He was in his swimming trunks, some loose khaki-coloured shorts with a drawstring, and his short-sleeved shirt was unbuttoned.

Jamie was confronted with a view of his muscled, bronzed torso, which was even more disconcerting than the bump on her forehead.

'What are *you* doing here?' she gasped, in the flimsy hope that her fuddled brain was playing tricks on her.

'Rescuing you again. I had no idea that you were so accident prone.' He reached out his hands to help her out. Jamie ignored him, choosing to swim to the steps in the shallow end and sit there, half immersed in the water.

'What were you thinking, swimming like greased lightning and not bothering to judge how far away the wall was?' Ryan shrugged off his shirt and settled into the water next to her. 'Here, let me have a look at that bump.'

'Let's not do this again,' Jamie snapped, touching the tender spot on her head and wincing. 'My head is fine, just as my feet were fine when I fell yesterday.'

'Bumps to the head can be far more serious. Tell me how many fingers I'm holding up.'

'I thought you were working,' she responded in an accusing voice, watching out of the corner of her eye as Ryan lounged back against the step behind him, resting on his elbows. His eyes were closed, his face tilted up to the sun and, like an addict, Jamie found herself watching him, taking in his powerful, masculine beauty. When he opened his eyes suddenly and glanced at her, she flushed and looked away.

'I *was* working, but I couldn't resist the thought of coming out here and having a dip. I didn't realise that you were such a strong swimmer.'

'Were you *watching* me?'

'Guilty as charged.' But he wouldn't let on for just how long. Nor would he let on that he had felt compelled to follow her out to the pool. For once in his life, he hadn't been able to concentrate on work. Watching her from above as she had whipped like a fish through the water had mesmerised him. Her bikini was a modest affair in black, the least obviously sexy swimsuit he had ever seen on a woman, and yet on her it was an erotic work of art. Sliding his eyes across, he took in the generous cleavage and the full swell of her ripe breasts—more than a generous, *very generous*, handful.

Just looking at her like this, with sexual hunger, was playing with fire. Ryan was getting dangerously close to the point of no longer caring whether she was his perfect secretary or not or whether going to bed with her would be crazy or not.

'Have you been in touch with your sister?'

'Have you forgotten that you broke my phone?'

'You'll be amply compensated for that the very second I get back to England. In fact, you're authorised to use company funds to get yourself the best mobile phone on the market as soon as *you* get back to England. No stinting!'

'That's very generous of you.'

'Well, it was my fault that you dropped your phone and broke it, although strictly speaking you should have listened to me in the first place and used the landline.'

'Funny the way you cause me to drop my phone and break it and yet it's still my fault.'

Ryan gave a rich chuckle. 'My mother says that you're the only woman she's ever met who can keep me in line. I think it was the way you accused me of cheating at Scrabble last night and insisted I remove my word and take a hefty penalty. And, hearing that acerbic tone of voice now, I'm inclined to agree.'

'And *I'm* sure that all those other women you dated would be inclined to disagree!'

'Have I ruffled your feathers? It was meant as a compliment. And just for the record, all those other women I dated were perfectly happy to let me take the lead. I can't think of any of them keeping me in line.'

'You haven't *ruffled my feathers*! And if any of them had worked for you…'

'Worked *with* me. We're a team, Jamie.'

'Well, whatever. If any of them had worked *with* you, then they'd find out soon enough that the only way to survive would be to try and…'

'Take control? I never thought that I would enjoy a woman who took control, bearing in mind my own disposition, but spending time with you here is certainly—'

'Useful!' Jamie interrupted hurriedly. 'I really hope that you're managing to accomplish all the work you set out to do.'

'It gets on my nerves when you do that.'

'When I do what?'

'And don't try that butter-wouldn't-melt-in-your-mouth routine. You know exactly what I'm talking about. The second the conversation veers off work, you frantically start trying to change the subject.'

'That's not true! I've chatted about all sorts of things with your family.'

'But not with me.'

'I'm not paid to chat about all sorts of things with you.' Jamie desperately tried to shove the genie back into the bottle.

'Are you scared of me? Is that it? Do I make you nervous?'

Jamie suddenly bristled. 'No, you don't make me nervous. But I know what's going on here—you're not accustomed to lazing around for days on end. I haven't known you take more than a weekend off work in all the time I've known you.'

'You've actually noticed?'

'Stop grinning! You're out here and maybe a little bored, so you're indulging yourself by...by confusing me.'

'Am I? I thought I was trying to get to know you.'

'You *already* know me.'

'Yes. I do, don't I?' Ryan murmured softly for, thinking about it, he did. Not the details; he had only just discovered that she had a sister. But he knew *her* in a weird sort of way. Working so closely with her, he had somehow tuned in to her personality. He knew how she responded to certain things, her mannerisms, her thoughts on a whole range of subjects from remarks she had made and which he had clearly absorbed over time. All this had built a picture lacking only in the detail. Like an itch he couldn't scratch, the thought of the vet being the privileged recipient of those details niggled at the back of his mind like a nasty irritant.

'As much as you must know me, my conscientious little secretary, which means that you must know that I don't want you holding off on contacting your sister because you feel awkward using the telephone here. Unless, of course, you don't want your conversations with the vet overheard by anyone. Or maybe you're embarrassed to be caught playing long-distance counsellor with a married man.'

'That's totally uncalled for!'

'Every time I mention the guy, you look guilty and embarrassed. Why is that?'

'You don't know what you're talking about.'

'I have eyes in my head. I'm telling you what I see.'

'You have absolutely no right to make suggestions like that!'

'I take it that's the guilt talking, because you sure as hell aren't answering my question. Was there something between the two of you? *Is* there still something between the two of you?'

'That's an insult!' Jamie pushed off from the step and began swimming furiously towards the other end of the pool, her one instinct just to get away from him.

She knew that he was right behind her when she reached the other end and heard the sound of him slicing through the water, but she refused to look around.

'Greg is married to my sister!' She fixed angry eyes on him as soon as he was next to her. 'There is *nothing* going on between us.'

'But he wasn't always married to your sister, was he? In fact, *you* knew him before your sister did. I saw the way you looked at him when he came through your front door on Christmas day...'

'That's ridiculous. I didn't look at him in any way.' Had she? Yes, of course she had. She had seen him for the first time in ages and at that point she hadn't even been sure that she had put her silly infatuation to rest. Slow colour crept into her face.

'Out of sight,' Ryan murmured, 'doesn't necessarily mean out of mind.'

Flustered, Jamie looked away but she could feel a nervous pulse racing at the base of her neck just as she was aware of his watchful eyes taking in every shadow of emotion she was desperately trying to conceal.

'Is that why you rushed down to London?'

'I came to London because...because I knew that it would be easier to find a job down here. Also, when Jessica got married, I sold our childhood home and split the proceeds with her. It gave me enough to put aside some savings for a place of my own, and sufficient for me to find somewhere to rent while I looked for work. It was just a...a matter of timing.'

'Why am I not buying that?'

'Because you have a suspicious mind.'

'Did you sleep with him?'

'That's outrageous!'

'Good.' So she hadn't. He gave her a slow, satisfied smile. 'Although I sense that any competition in that area wouldn't be worth worrying about.'

'What are you saying?'

'Read between the lines. What do you think I'm saying?' Ryan didn't know when he had made the decision to overstep the mark. He just knew that he wanted her. The control that he had always been able to access when it came to women had disappeared under the force of a craving that seemed to have crept up on him only to pounce, taking him by surprise and demolishing every scrap of common sense in its voracious path.

He didn't give himself time to think. He also didn't give *her* time to think. In one smooth motion, he circled her, trapping her to the side of the pool by the effective measure of placing his hands on either side of her. He leant into her, felt her breath against his face, read the panic in her eyes that couldn't quite extinguish the simmering excitement. He had been right all along when he had sensed her forbidden interest in him and the knowledge gave him a rock-hard erection even before his lips touched hers.

Nothing had ever felt this good. That brief, public kiss they had shared at Christmas had been just a taster. Her mouth parted on a moan and, while her hands scrabbled against his chest in protest, the feel of her tongue against his was telling a different story.

He pushed her back against the wall so that his big body was pressed firmly against hers. The bottom of the pool sloped slightly upwards at this end and, standing at a little over six-two, Ryan was steady and balanced on his feet. For Jamie to keep her balance, however, she had to hook both her arms up on the wooden planks, which threw her breasts into tempting prominence. She attempted to say something and he killed the words forming on her tongue by deepening his kiss. Her eyes were half-closed. When she broke free to tilt her head back, he trailed his tongue against the slender column of her neck and Jamie shuddered in instant reaction.

More than anything else, she wanted to push him away but her will power had self-imploded and her body was as limp as a rag doll's as she soaked up the amazing feelings zipping through her as if a million shooting stars had been released inside her body.

She was dimly aware of him reaching down to hook her legs around his waist, and the nudge of his erection between her spread legs brought her close to swooning.

Water sloshed over the side of the pool as they moved frantically against each other. When he pulled down the straps of her bikini, she was self-conscious but only for a brief moment, then that, like her inhibitions, disappeared completely. With her body arched back and angled half out of the water, the touch of his mouth on her nipple was exquisite as the hot sun blazed down on them.

She could have stayed like this for ever, with him suckling on her breasts, massaging them with his big hands, rolling her nipples between his fingers and then teasing them with his tongue into hard, sensitised peaks.

It was only when he began to tug down her bikini bottom so that he could slide his fingers into her that Jamie's eyes flew open and she took horrified stock of the reality of what she was doing.

How on earth had this happened?

Of course, she knew. Why kid herself? She had been lusting after him for months—indeed, it felt like for ever. This was nothing at all like what she had felt for Greg. Not only had Ryan ignited something in her that had never been ignited before, but it was all the more powerful because it was wrapped up in a package that was more than just physical attraction. The whole complex, three-dimensional person had swept her off her feet. She hadn't even known that she had been carried away until now.

She wriggled, pushing him away from her, and then ducked under his hands so that she could swim away with frantic, urgent speed towards the far end of the pool.

Ryan easily caught up with her.

'What the hell is the matter?'

Jamie couldn't meet his eyes but she had to when she felt his fingers on her chin and was roughly made to look at him.

'I…I don't know what happened,' she whispered.

'That's fine because *I* know what happened and I'm more than happy to explain it to you. We're attracted to one another. I touched you and you went up in flames.'

'I didn't!'

'Stop pretending, Jamie. Why did you stop?'

'Because it's…it's wrong.'

She wasn't saying anything that took him by surprise. Only twenty-four hours ago he had thought about her and dismissed any notion of getting her into his bed as flat-out crazy. Yet here he was, and it didn't feel crazy.

'We're adults,' he growled. 'We're permitted to be turned on by each other.'

'You're my boss. I work for you!'

'I want more than your diligence. I want you in my bed where I can touch you wherever I want. I'm betting that that's what you want too, whether you think it's right or wrong. In fact, I'm betting that if I touch you right now, right here…' Ryan trailed his finger along her cleavage and watched as she fought to catch her breath '…you're not going to be able to tell me that you don't want me too.'

'I don't want you.'

'Liar!' He kissed her again and her lies were revealed in

the way she clutched at him, not wanting to but utterly unable to resist.

Jamie felt her weakness tearing her apart. Her mouth blindly responded and she missed his lips when he pulled back to look at her.

'*Now* tell me that you just don't know what came over you.'

'Okay. Okay. Maybe I'm attracted to you, but I'm not proud of it.' The words felt agonisingly painful and she twisted away from his piercing gaze. 'I... You're right, okay? I felt things for Greg. That's why it was important to leave, to live somewhere else, somewhere far away.' This felt like the final confession. She was now waving goodbye to her privacy for ever, but what was her option? She had to dig deep and find the strength to turn away from him with a good excuse because if she didn't he would devour her. She knew that.

Ryan had stilled. For a minute, his stomach twisted into a sickening knot. So she might not have slept with the vet, but she had felt something for him, maybe even loved him. He was shaken by the impact that her admission had on him.

'I made a mistake with Greg and I've learnt from it. I haven't come this far to make a second mistake. I won't climb into bed with you just for the hell of it. I'm going to go and I want you to promise me that you'll never mention this again.'

'What a lot of things I'm now under orders never to mention,' Ryan rasped in a savage undertone. 'And who ever said that sex between us would be a mistake?'

'I did.' This time she met his eyes squarely. 'I'm not like you. I'm not willing to fall in and out with bed with someone just because I fancy them. If you don't think that you can put this behind us, then I'm telling you right now that

I'll have my resignation waiting for you on your desk when you return to England from Florida.'

This wasn't a veiled threat, she meant every word of it; Ryan mentally cursed to himself. He had always accepted his ability to win women over. Jamie felt like the first woman he had ever really wanted and she was turning him down. Frustration ripped through him and he clenched his fists but there was nothing to say.

She was waiting for confirmation and he nodded curtly and in silence.

'Good.' Her body was still burning, but she had rescued what she could of her dignity. It felt like a very small victory. 'I'll head inside now.' She stepped out of the water and tried not to think of his hands all over her and his mouth lingering on her breasts. It had happened and it wasn't going to happen again. Just for good measure, and to show him that she meant business, she shot him one final look over her shoulder. 'Is there anything you'd like me to be getting on with?'

'Why don't you use your initiative?' Ryan said coolly. 'I would suggest something suitably engrossing that can help you forget this sordid little business of sexual attraction.'

On the tip of his tongue was the temptation to tell her that perhaps the vet *had* ended up with the wrong sister. Jamie didn't want a real man. She didn't want to be sexually challenged. No wonder she had fallen in love with a guy whose top priority was his sick animals with everything else taking second place. How demanding would a relationship with him be? Not very. Which would have suited his prim, efficient secretary right down to the ground.

And that closing thought should have made him feel a lot better as he watched her walk away with her towel firmly secured around her waist, but it didn't.

In fact, he felt a distinct urge to bash something very hard.

Instead, he made do with the pool. He swam with intensity, not looking up, until the muscles in his arms began to burn and the sun began its descent. He had no idea how long he did it. He was a prodigiously strong swimmer but even for him over two hours without rest began to take its toll.

Nevertheless, he might have continued swimming, slackening his pace, if he wasn't distracted by the sound of footsteps—running footsteps.

In the tropics, night fell quickly, preceded only by a window of blazing orange when the sun dipped below the horizon. The sky was orange now. Soon, it would be replaced by deep, velvety charcoal-black, but in the fading light he made out Jamie's slight figure as she paused at the top of the steps and then began running down them.

No wonder the woman had so many accidents!

Ryan heaved himself out of the water and without bothering to dry himself slung on the shirt which he had earlier discarded.

'Urgent work problem?' he asked sarcastically, and then paused when his eyes focused on her face and he took in her expression. She was panicked and her panic was contagious. He felt a sudden cold chill of apprehension. 'What is it? What's the matter?'

'It's your mother, Ryan. Something's wrong with her.'

'What are you talking about?' But he was already heading away from the pool, half running and half turning so that Jamie could talk to him.

'I had a shower, and when I couldn't find her anywhere I thought I'd check her bedroom to find out whether she wanted a cup of tea. When I went in, she was lying on the bed, white as a sheet. She said that she's had some tingling in her arms, Ryan, and her breathing's erratic. I rushed down here as fast as I could...'

They were at the house and Ryan was taking the stairs

two at a time, while Jamie raced behind him, out of breath in her haste to keep up. She must have been gone all of five minutes, if that, and she hoped, as she nearly catapulted Ryan in the doorway to the bedroom, that his mother had had a miraculous recovery. That all those little signs were no more than a bout of extreme exhaustion.

Vivian Sheppard was awake but obviously unwell and extremely frightened.

Within seconds, Ryan was on the phone to the hospital. The strings he was capable of pulling were not limited to his homeland; Jamie listened as he urgently asked for a specific consultant, watched as he nodded, satisfied with whatever reply he received.

'The ambulance will be here in five minutes.' He knelt by the bed and took his mother's hand in his own. Vivian, usually sprightly and full of laughter, was drawn but still managing to smile weakly at her son.

'I'm sure there's nothing to worry about,' she murmured and tut-tutted when he told her not to speak.

Behind him, Jamie hovered uncertainly, feeling like an intruder at a very private moment. She longed to see his face and desperately wanted to comfort him, but she kept her hands stiffly behind her back. As soon as she picked up the sound of the approaching ambulance, she ran downstairs and directed them to Vivian's bedroom.

To remain behind or to accompany them in the ambulance? Rather than impose an awkward situation on Ryan, who was grey with worry, she quietly informed him that she would stay at the house but would remain up until he returned.

'I can't tell you when that will be,' Ryan said, barely looking at her as he shoved on a tee-shirt and stuck his feet in his loafers.

'It's okay.'

'Thank God you went in to check in on her.'

Jamie placed her hand on his arm and felt the heat of his body through the dry tee-shirt. It took a lot to keep her hand there and not whip it away as though it had been burnt.

'I know you must be worried sick, but try not to be. Worry is contagious. You don't want your mother thinking the worst.'

'You're right,' Ryan agreed heavily. 'Look, I have to go. I'll phone the landline as soon as I can. Or better still…' he flicked out his mobile phone and handed it to her '…take this. I'll use my mother's phone to call you.'

Then he was gone, and in a heartbeat the sound of the ambulance siren was fading in the distance until the only sounds she could hear, once again, were the crickets and other night-time insects and the soft breeze sifting through the trees and shrubs.

Over the next three hours, she sat on the sofa in the living room with the windows open and a gentle breeze blowing back the white muslin curtains. His mobile was right there, on the small rattan table next to her, but it didn't ring. She must have dozed off; she was awakened by the sound of the front door slamming, then the sound of footsteps, and then Ryan was standing at the door to the room before she had much of a chance to gather herself.

'I thought you were going to call,' she said sleepily, shoving herself into an upright position on the sofa. 'I was worried. How is your mother doing? Is she going to be all right? What is the prognosis?'

Ryan walked towards her and sat on the sofa, depressing it with his weight and bringing her fractionally closer to him in the process.

'A minor stroke. The consultant says that there's nothing to worry about.'

'But you're still looking worried.'

'Can you blame me?' He leant forward and rested his head in his hands for a few moments, letting the silence settle between them. Then he looked at her and her heartbeat quickened because every instinct in her wanted to reach out and draw him to her so that she could smooth away the lines of worry on his face.

'Anyway, they did a number of tests on her, and they're going to keep her in for a couple of days so that they can do some more, but it's all very reassuring.'

'Did they say what caused it?'

'One of those things.' That was what had been said to him. Personally, he put it down to stress, and here things got a little difficult because what was there for his mother to stress about? She lived a relaxed and comfortable life. The only thing she had ever been known to worry about had been her children, and with Claire, Hannah and Susie all settled and happy with their respective broods *he* was the only one left for her to be concerned about.

Over the past few hours, while he had sat on a hard chair in the hospital waiting for doctors to return with results of tests, Ryan had had time to think.

His mother had been worrying more and more over the past couple of years about his singleton status, the women he dated and the hours he worked. Had she been more anxious about it than she had let on? While he had been travelling the world, working all the hours God made and fitting in his no-strings attached relationships with sexy airheads, had she been fretting to the point that her health had suffered? He was assailed by guilt.

'Have you been in touch with your sisters?' He didn't want to talk. His silence was leaden and he was obviously a million miles away in his head. For some reason, that was painfully disappointing. Jamie wanted him to turn to her and she had to mentally slap herself on the wrist for her foolish weakness. It was as if a door in her mind had been unlocked and flung open and now that it had been she was besieged by frightening and unwelcome revelations about herself and the way she felt about him.

When she was beginning to think that she should go to bed, because she was clearly an inconvenience when he just wanted to be by himself, he looked up at her.

'I phoned Hannah and explained the situation. Of course she wanted to get straight back on a plane over, but I managed to persuade her that there would be no point. I will stay here until my mother is fit to travel and then I will return to the UK with her.' He hesitated and for the first time he focused fully on the woman sitting next to him.

'You'll have to cancel my trip to Florida. Get in touch with the office. Either Evans or George Law can handle it. Email them whatever information they need.'

Jamie nodded. He was still looking at her as though there was more to be said but he wasn't quite sure how to say it. Maybe, she thought, he was embarrassed to have her there when this family crisis was happening. Maybe he wanted her to leave immediately but was uncertain how to frame the request, considering it had been his idea to have her tag along with him in the first place.

'Of-of course,' she stammered, chewing on her lower lip. 'And…just to tell you that you shouldn't be, you know, embarrassed because you want me to leave. I absolutely and fully understand. What's happened is completely unexpected and the last thing you need is for me to be here. This isn't a time for your secretary to be hanging around getting in the way.' She tried a reassuring smile on for size. 'I'd probably feel exactly the same if the roles were reversed and you were *my* secretary.'

Her attempt to lighten the strained atmosphere fell flatter than a lead balloon but after a few seconds he did manage to give her a crooked smile.

'I think you've got hold of the wrong end of the stick,' he said eventually. 'I'm not sure how to tell you this...'

'Tell me what?' For the first time, Jamie felt a stab of real apprehension. The incident by the pool resurfaced in her mind and she cringed at the memory: that was the reason for his hesitation. He had had the chance to reflect on their inappropriate behaviour and now had come the moment of reckoning. Tears of bitter regret pushed their way to the back of her eyes as she envisaged her wonderful, well paid, satisfying job disappearing like a puff of smoke in the air.

CHAPTER SEVEN

RYAN continued to look at her. She had obviously fallen asleep on the chair; her cheeks were flushed and her hair was tousled. She looked young and innocent and nothing at all like the businesslike, crisp, efficient secretary he had become accustomed to. But then hadn't he seen the living, breathing, exciting woman behind the professional persona?

He reined back his imagination which would break free and gallop away. Right now, he needed to focus, because the conversation that lay ahead was probably going to be difficult.

'I honestly don't know how to say this…'

'I can't imagine you're ever stuck for words.' This was sounding worse by the second.

'My mother saw us. By the pool. Earlier today.'

'Oh, no.' Jamie put her hand to her mouth in dismay. Hot colour spread across her cheeks. 'How do you know? Did she tell you?'

'Of course she told me. I didn't use my imagination to work out a possible scenario. She decided to go for a little stroll around the gardens to see if some fresh air would give her more energy and she heard us. She followed the sound of our voices and I think she got a bit more than she bargained for.'

'I'm sorry. This is all my fault!' Suddenly there was no

part of her that could keep still and Jamie stood up to wander agitatedly around the room. She had to clasp her hands together to stop them from trembling and the wave of shameful discomfort was like a thousand painful burrs underneath her skin.

'I'll leave immediately.' She went to stand in front of him and drew in her breath to fortify herself against the mortification of meeting his eyes. 'It'll take me half an hour to pack.'

'Oh, for God's sake, don't be absurd!'

'I can't stay here. I don't think I'd be able to look your mother in the face. What we did was terrible. A mistake. She must have been appalled. Is that why...? Did we cause...?'

'No! Now sit *down*!' He waited until she was seated, although she still looked as though she would have liked to flee through the open door. 'What she saw didn't cause her to go into some kind of meltdown. My mother is pretty liberated when it comes to her children and what they get up to, believe me. In fact...'

'In fact *what*? I wish you'd just say what you have to say, Ryan. I'm a big girl. I can take bad news.'

'In fact, my mother was overjoyed at what she witnessed before she walked back to the house, no doubt with a smile on her face.'

'I'm sorry, but I don't know what you're saying.'

'I'm saying, Jamie, that my mother, as I've told you, has been, shall we say, anxious about my lifestyle for quite some time. I have no idea why, but there you go. The harridans have assured me that it's because I'm her only son and the baby of the family. At any rate, she saw us and she's jumped to certain conclusions.'

'What conclusions?' Jamie asked, totally bewildered by this point.

'That we're somehow involved.'

'We are. I work for you.'

'Strangely, seeing me all over you at the side of the pool didn't point to that particular conclusion. I've always maintained a healthy distance from the women who have worked for me in the past.'

'Involved?' Jamie squeaked, horrified.

'As in, an item. As in, romantically connected. As in...'

'I get the picture!'

'I'm not sure that you do, actually. My mother is under the impression that I've been too sheepish to say anything because I've always made a big deal of keeping my work life separate from my private life. In her wild and inventive imagination, we've only managed to keep our hands off one another while my sisters and their brood were around, but the second they all left we just couldn't help ourselves, it would seem.'

Jamie put her hands to her cheeks, which were burning hot. 'And did you tell her the truth?'

'Well, now here comes the tricky part...'

Ryan allowed a few moments of silence, during which he hoped she would join the dots and read what he was trying to say without him having to spell it out in black and white, but for once it seemed like her fine mind had deserted her.

'I couldn't,' he finally said bluntly.

'What do you mean *you couldn't*?'

'My mother has taken a shine to you. She's met a few of my girlfriends in the past and they haven't come up to her exacting standards.'

Distracted, Jamie couldn't resist the temptation to mutter under her breath that some of the girlfriends *she* had met would have fallen short of most mothers' standards, even if the standards weren't particularly exacting.

'She seems to think that we're involved in a serious relationship. I couldn't disillusion her because she's just had a stroke, albeit a mild one, and the last thing I want is for her to be subjected to any unnecessary stress. Not to put too fine a point on it, her last words before they wheeled her off for the first series of tests were that she was overjoyed that I had finally come to my senses and found myself a woman who could keep up with me.'

'This is awful!' Suddenly Jamie was really, really angry. Not only had she made a horrendous mistake—thrown away her precious privacy, engaged in wildly inappropriate behaviour and, worse, allowed herself feelings for a man who had no feelings for her—but now she was effectively being told that she wouldn't be able to put the whole sorry episode behind her because his mother had jumped to all the wrong conclusions and Ryan had made no effort to enlighten her.

'I appreciate that your mother doesn't need additional stress, Ryan, but it's going to be even more stressful for her if you deceive her over this and then have to tell her the truth when she's back on her feet. She'll never trust you again!'

'So you think that I should take the risk of damaging her health to be honest, do you? Do you imagine that you're the only person with a sense of family responsibility? My father died and my mother became the lynchpin of the family. She's been through a hell of a lot! She's had to cope with the shock of realising that the family finances had become a joke. She's had to suffer through tough times when so-called friends dropped by the wayside because she was no longer living in a big house and driving a big car.'

'And you had to witness all of that. How awful for you. I'm so sorry, Ryan. Truly I am.'

'We all have our stories to tell. Jamie! I was there to pick up the pieces, and when it comes to my mother's health and her peace of mind I'm not going anywhere. I'm still going to be here to pick up the pieces.'

It was shocking to see the lines of pain and worry etched

on his face. The Ryan who could take on the world and win was letting down his guard. Behind the dominant, powerful male, she had a glimpse of the confused boy who was forced to grow up fast. As she had.

'So I let my mother have the luxury of believing what she wanted to believe.'

'I...'

'You know what, Jamie? Perhaps you're right. Perhaps it would be better for you to leave. I'm sure I'll be able to explain your absence to my mother.'

In possession of what she thought she had wanted, Jamie found that she was now reluctant to leave. Ryan adored his family; he didn't have to verbalise it. Right now, he looked drained and so unlike the vibrant man she knew that her heart felt as though it was tearing in two. She knew that he wouldn't try to stop her if she decided to take him up on his offer and walk away, but their relationship would be irrevocably changed for ever. Would she even be able to continue working for him?

And why was she so angry at the thought of giving in to what he wanted? His mother was ill, and if a piece of harmless fiction would allow her to recover more quickly then where was the crime in that? They would return to London and in due course Ryan would gently break the news that they had broken up, amicably of course, and his mother would probably be sorry to hear it but her health certainly wouldn't suffer. Whereas now, still vulnerable, what if she *did* react badly? She was old and old people could be strangely fragile when it came to certain things, when it came to the well-being of their loved ones.

With a sickening jolt of self-awareness, Jamie knew why she was angry. Her anger stemmed from fear, whatever excuse she chose to hide behind, and her fear stemmed from the fact that Ryan had become far more than a boss to her.

She had feelings for him, and she might just as well have dug a hole for herself, jumped in and begun shovelling the earth over her head. She didn't want the pretence of being involved with Ryan because she was scared that the lines between fact and fiction might become blurred, scared that she would be left damaged, that the fiction would not be harmless after all, at least not to her.

Stuck between a rock and a hard place, Jamie navigated her way through a series of grim scenarios and, like a drowning person finally breaking the surface of the water, found the one and only way she could justify going along with his crazy idea and breathed a sigh of heady relief. She would treat it as a business proposition. He wanted her to play a pretend game, having no idea how dangerous for her the game could be, and she would box the pretence into a neat, controllable package and coolly look at it as just another part of her job.

'What exactly would this pretence entail?'

'Are you saying that you're willing to go along with me? It's a big ask, Jamie. I know that and, believe me, I would be very grateful indeed. But if you decide to jump in feet first then you can't decide halfway through that you'd really prefer the moral high-ground.'

'I'm taking it that this charade would only be appropriate while we're out here with your mother?'

'Naturally.'

'Which would be how long, exactly?'

'At least another week. I'm pretty confident that she will be able to travel back to the UK by then. She might even be able to travel back before, but I'm not into taking risks when it comes to my family.' He gave her a crooked smile, and Jamie tried to maintain a professional distance by not smiling back at him, although she could feel the hairs on the back of her neck stand on end. 'I've always saved my risk taking for the work arena.'

'Another week.' Jamie stared off into the distance and tried to break down the week into smaller, more manageable segments. Seven days during which there would be long periods of time in which there would be no need to pretend anything because his mother would probably be asleep or resting. 'Right,' she said crisply. 'I'll agree, on the condition that we get one thing perfectly straight.'

'And what might that be?'

'What happened out there by the pool was a terrible mistake.' Jamie looked at him squarely and directly. 'The sun, these exotic surroundings... Well, it was a moment of madness in unfamiliar surroundings and, yes, of course you're an attractive man. Things happened that shouldn't have happened. But I need your word that, if we're to pretend to be something we aren't for the sake of your mother, nothing physical must happen again. In other words, there must be very clear boundaries between us.'

A lull of silence greeted this remark, as thick and as heavy as treacle. Ryan's dark, inscrutable eyes resting lazily on her face made it difficult to hold on to her composure and she could feel tension coiling inside her, trickling through every part of her nerve-wracked body. Only a lifetime's habit of keeping her emotions to herself allowed her to maintain his gaze without flinching.

'Is that speech directed at yourself as well?'

'What do you mean?'

'I'm not some kind of arch seducer, lurking behind walls, waiting to pounce on an innocent victim. Sexual attraction is a funny thing in my experience. It hardly ever responds to the calm voice of reason.'

'Perhaps in your case, but certainly not in mine.'

'Maybe,' Ryan murmured, 'if you had ditched the virtue

and flung yourself at the vet he might have married a different sister.'

And just like that, he had changed the tenor of the conversation. With a single flick of the finger, he had overturned the pedestal on which she had valiantly sought to place herself, safely out of reach. Jamie's skin burned as she contemplated the awkward question that he had dragged out into the open.

How was it that she had never, not once, been really tempted to put her attraction to Greg to the test? How had it been so easy to restrain herself around him when with Ryan, a far more unsuitable and inappropriate candidate for her affections, she had gone up in flames, had found it impossible to rein back her frantic, screaming urge to touch him and to let him touch her? Was he now wondering the same thing? Would she be condemned now to always play the role of the woman who couldn't resist him? When they returned to England, and he resumed his life with the blonde bimbos and the airhead catwalk queens, would he still be smirking to himself that his quiet little secretary was lusting after him as she ducked behind her computer? Galling thought!

'Maybe I respond to you,' Jamie returned sharply. 'But I was thinking of Greg! Maybe it was all just a piece of weird, delayed emotional transference.'

'You used me as a substitute, in other words? Is that what you're saying?'

'I'm saying that there's no point analysing anything. What happened happened, but it's not going to happen again, and I need your word on that or else I won't agree to any charade. You needn't worry about me and those ideas you have about sexual attraction. I can handle myself.'

So, Ryan thought with slow-building murderous rage the likes of which he had never felt before, when she had arched back and succumbed to the sensation of his tongue gently caressing her nipple while the water lapped warmly around them had she actually been seeing the vet's face in her mind's eye? Ryan had never had much time for psycho-babble but he could grudgingly see that the sudden appear-ance of the vet might have kick started something in her that had culminated in the temporary breaking down of her inhibitions with him. And he didn't like it.

'You have my word.' He smiled grimly and stood up. 'We should both get some sleep now. It's late. I'll be leaving for the hospital first thing in the morning.'

'Would…would it be okay if I came along with you? I've grown very fond of your mother in the short time I've known her. I'd like to see how she's doing for myself.'

Ryan began heading for the door. There was no point dwelling on the unsavoury possibility that he had been used as a substitute for someone else, that he had been the wrong boss, in the wrong place at the wrong time. He resisted the unnatural urge to worry the remark to death until he suc-ceeded in extracting some alternative, more favourable ex-planation for the way she had responded to him. Instead, he locked the door on those unsettling thoughts and half-turned to find her right behind him.

Switching off the light, the room was suddenly plunged into semi-darkness but he could still make out the anxious glitter in her eyes. Whatever murky water happened to be flowing underneath their respective bridges at the moment, there was no doubt that she cared about his mother.

'There's no point, really. I'll tell her that you wanted to visit, but she'll be back here within a day or so and you can tell her for yourself. Your time would be better spent here, seeing to all the rearrangements that will have to be put in motion for the meetings in Florida. You'll need to make sure that all the relevant information gets emailed to George

Law. He would be a better bet to cover for me than Evans, I think. He might even find all those graphs and flip charts you prepared a handy tool.'

Jamie felt tears prick the corners of her eyes. She had to look away quickly and was grateful for the relative darkness. This was the Ryan she found so sweetly irresistible—the teasing, laid-back Ryan—and when that side of him went into retreat it was as if a dark cloud had settled over her world.

'You were never going to use any of them, were you?' she queried lightly, knowing that they were both attempting to find some of the familiar ground they had lost.

'I would have taken them all with me. As for using them, well, my speeches tend to be of the "winging it" variety, although that chart with all the different colours was very appealing.'

'I'll make sure that everything is sorted out,' Jamie promised, stepping into the hall and closing the door behind her.

'I'm sure you will. I have every faith in you.'

There was no need to dwell any longer on the dos and dont's of the strange game upon which she had agreed to embark.

As it turned out, she had less time to worry over it because Vivian was released the following day.

Jamie, having put through the final call to one of the senior conference organisers in Florida, was leaving the office at a little after five in the afternoon when she heard the sound of Ryan's car drawing up on the drive outside.

He had been out of the house since eight-thirty, calling only to tell her that he intended to stay in the town and use his time meeting with one of the head honchos of the tourist board so that he could throw around a few ideas he had had about the possibility of opening a boutique hotel on the island. Jamie knew that he had been playing around with the notion of extending the boundaries of his empire over the past few months, and she wasn't surprised that he would choose the island which he knew intimately.

She had no idea how the rest of the evening would evolve, and her stomach clenched into nervous knots as she headed towards the front door. But when it was pushed open she saw Vivian, pale but looking much healthier than before, preceding her son into the airy, flagstone open area.

'Darling girl, I'm so pleased to see you.'

Jamie walked into a warm embrace and managed to catch Ryan's eye over his mother's shoulder.

'How are you feeling, Vivian?'

'Like an old woman.' She dismissed it with a smile, linking her arm through Jamie's and walking towards the sitting room, which was one of the coolest rooms in the house thanks to the expanse of French doors which could be flung open to admit the balmy breezes, and the overhead ceiling fan. 'I thought that I was as healthy as a horse,' she confided, settling herself on the striped sofa where she suddenly looked much more frail. 'But don't we all, until something comes along to remind us that we aren't? Thankfully, my stroke was very, very mild. A warning, the doctor told me. I need to start slowing down.' She closed her eyes briefly and then opened them to smile at her son who had taken up position behind Jamie.

His hand was curved lightly on the nape of her neck and she was acutely conscious of the gentle stroking of his thumb on her skin. So this was what the charade felt like—a casual intimacy which his mother would expect of two people who were an item, and which was devastating on her senses.

Vivian was a smaller, softer, rounder version of her son. The same dark hair, the same dark eyes. These dark eyes were now happily taking them both in.

'My darling,' she said warmly. 'I can't tell you how thrilled I was when Ryan explained the situation.'

Jamie edged away from those disturbing fingers to sit on one of the upright chairs, leaving Ryan to sink onto the sofa next to his mother, conveniently no longer within touching distance. She tentatively touched the back of her neck where it still tingled, and pinned an engaging smile on her face.

'He's been a naughty boy. There was no need for the cloak-and-dagger routine. Of course, we all know how firm he's always been about keeping his love life—'

'Mother! I'm right here!'

Vivian patted his knee fondly but her eyes remained on Jamie. 'I know, and that's why I refrained from saying your *sex* life.'

Ryan groaned and flushed darkly. It was a pinprick of the comic in an awkward situation, if only Vivian knew.

'Away from the office, but I couldn't be more delighted. He must have told you that I've been worrying for some time now that he needs to find himself a good woman and settle down.'

'It's been mentioned,' Jamie murmured when she realised that an answer was expected of her, and Vivian greeted that acknowledgement with a beam of satisfied approval.

'Knowing that he has has made all the difference. I'm certain I'm back on my feet so quickly simply because I'm just so happy!'

Over the course of the next hour and a half, Vivian swatted aside enquiries about her nutrition regime, exercise plan and plans for when she returned to England in favour of the more absorbing topic of her son's good fortune in finding Jamie. She asked questions which brought a rush of embarrassed colour and tongue-tied silence to Jamie but which Ryan, Oscar-winning actor that he seemed to be, answered with aplomb.

She wondered aloud at her amazing ability to read a situation, exclaiming that she had just guessed from the *very start* that something was up by the way her son looked at Jamie. She blushed delicately when she referred to that moment when her suspicions had been confirmed, having accidentally spied them kissing at the side of the pool. She hastened to add that she had not lingered and so had witnessed nothing beyond 'a passionate kiss that said it all', while Jamie wished for the ground to open and swallow her up, hopefully to disgorge her into a world where the events of the past few weeks had never happened.

Vivian retired to bed with a light supper of tea and toast, leaving Jamie to glumly contemplate the mess into which they had both managed to get themselves.

'This,' she announced, as soon as Ryan was back in the sitting room, 'is a nightmare.'

'We'll discuss this outside. I no longer trust my mother not to pop up in unexpected places, and she doesn't need to have her high hopes dashed by a few careless words from you.'

He turned on his heel and she dashed behind him out onto the veranda, and then away completely from the house as they manoeuvred down the hill via a series of twisting wooden steps until they emerged onto the white, sandy beach below.

It was dark, but out here, under a full moon, the sea glinted and glittered like a placid lake of slick, black oil.

It was only the third time Jamie had actually been on the beach, and the first time at night, and she marvelled at its spectacular isolation. The house was very cleverly situated atop a natural, protected cove which could only be accessed by boat or via the grounds of the house, which were private property. Thus, it was perfectly peaceful. Bits of driftwood were scattered here and there, and the husks of fallen coconuts had been a never-ending source of fun and play for the little ones when they had been at the house. Ryan stooped to pick one up now and absently threw it out to sea in a long, wide arc before moving to sit on the sand, out of the reach of the sea gently lapping on the shore.

'I had no idea your mother was so...'

'Taken with the idea of you and I?'

'I was going to say desperate to see you settled down.'

'Are you saying that only a desperate man would choose you to settle down with?' He lay back on the sand with his hands folded behind his head and Jamie flounced down next to him, although sitting up so that she could glare at his face.

'That's not what I'm saying,' she denied in frustration. 'What on earth are we going to do?'

'We've already been over this.'

'I hadn't thought it through. I hadn't realised that we would have to build a great detailed story of how we...we...'

'Fell into each other's arms? Were drawn to one another over the coffee machine and the filing cabinets?'

'How can you think that it's funny? Your mother really believes that we're on the verge of announcing our engagement!'

'Now you're beginning to realise the position I was in when I found myself having to humour her. In her fragile condition, the last thing I could have done would have been to announce that we were involved in a little light-hearted hanky panky. I'm afraid she sees you as someone far too decent and moral and responsible to get carried away by lust, which would have left her thinking that I had seduced you for a bit of passing fun, only to toss you aside the second I was through with you.'

'You mean the way you usually treat the women you've been out with?'

'I refuse to be baited into an argument. This is the reality we're dealing with. I explained the situation to you and you signed up to the deal.'

'Yes, but I didn't sign up to any physical contact. You know that.'

He continued staring up, and to get his attention before her frustration ran away with her Jamie gathered some sand in her fist and slapped it down on his chest.

Quick as a flash, and before she could even think of taking avoidance tactics, his hand was curled round her wrist and he half sat up, propping himself up by his elbow.

'We're lovers, remember? My mother might be old but she's not away with the fairies. Keeping a healthy distance and smiling politely is going to set the alarm bells going in her head.'

'Yes, but—'

'But *what*? I touched you for three seconds on the nape of your neck. I wasn't plunging my hands down your tee-shirt!'

Jamie squirmed. His fingers were like a steel vice around her wrist, burning a hole in her skin.

'Why don't you pretend that I'm the vet?' he gritted savagely. 'Then you might start enjoying the occasional passing touch.'

She squeezed her eyes shut. She should never have implied that she had used him, should never have implied that she had been fired up by thoughts of Greg when Ryan had been touching her in the pool. That had been an outright lie, and afterwards she had felt like a coward who was happy to shunt the blame for her behaviour onto someone else because it was easier than having to accept responsibility for her own actions—misguided, stupid or otherwise.

She would not have liked it if a man had touched her intimately and she had responded to his touch, only to be told that she had been nothing but a fill-in for the woman he really wanted but couldn't have.

'That wouldn't work,' she confessed in a tight voice. 'Now, please let me go.'

Ryan released her immediately. He didn't know what the hell had prompted him to drag the vet into the conversation. He had determined to put that unpleasant conversation of earlier behind him and move on. Evidently, it had continued to prey on his mind.

'What's that supposed to mean?' He sat up and watched her narrowly as she massaged her wrist.

'I shouldn't have said what I said about... Sorry, I shouldn't have implied that you were a substitute for Greg. I've discovered that I put Greg behind me a lot longer ago than I thought.'

'Go on.'

'To what? There's nothing else to say. If I gave the wrong impression to you, then I apologise.'

'Let me get this straight.' Ryan only became aware of his black mood now that it was in the process of vanishing. 'You don't get turned on at the thought of the vet?'

'It would seem not.'

'So by the pool, that hot response really *was* all for me?'

'That still doesn't mean that it was right! What we did...'

'And you don't want any physical contact because I turn you on and you don't like that.'

'Something along those lines,' Jamie muttered, hot all over and agonisingly conscious of his glittering dark eyes fixed like laser beams on her face. 'I should tell you what I managed to sort out on the work front. I haven't had a chance, what with everything this evening.'

But, while her head was telling her that that was the best route away from this uncomfortable topic, her addled brain was refusing to go along for the ride.

Ryan tilted his head obligingly to one side. God, he suddenly felt on top of the world. He must have an ego as tough as an egg shell, he thought wryly, if a few insinuations and ill-chosen words from a woman who wasn't even his lover could reduce him to an ill-tempered bore. And if a retraction could reverse the effect in a heartbeat.

'You spoke to Law?' he prompted.

'And emailed all the info over. And…um…' Jamie licked her lips. 'I also contacted all the relevant people in, um, Florida.'

'And? Um? Ah, um…'

'You're making fun of me!'

'I'm intrigued by your sudden attack of nerves.'

'Can you blame me?'

Ryan didn't pretend to misunderstand her. 'No. No, I can't. You owned up to something you found difficult and I admire you for that. It was a brave thing to do. I'll keep all physical contact to the minimum, of course. If that's what you want.'

'It is.' Even to her own ears, she could hear the telltale waver in her voice.

'Okay, I won't touch you, but feel free to touch *me*,' he said in a husky undertone. 'Any time you like and anywhere you like because I'm happy to admit that you make me feel like a randy teenager. In fact, right now I'm hot for you, and I won't run screaming like an outraged virgin if you decide to touch me and feel for yourself.'

He hadn't just thrown down the challenge, he had hurled it like a javelin, and it lay between them now, waiting for her to decide what to do with it.

'Why do you have to make me laugh? It's not fair.' Jamie's breathing was shallow and painful and she leaned forward, resting on her outstretched hands, already knowing what she would do with that hurled challenge.

'Life seldom is. If you want me, you have to reach out and touch me.'

'Just while we're here,' she said on a soft moan. Of its own accord, her hand reached out to curl into the opening of his shirt, between two buttons, so that her knuckles were brushing his chest. 'Just for this week. If we can pretend to be something we're not for the sake of your mother, let's just pretend to be different people to one another. I won't be your secretary. You won't be my boss. Just for a few days, can we simply be two people, strangers who happened to meet on a very beautiful island in the Caribbean? Can we?'

'We'll pretend whatever you want,' Ryan growled. 'Now, take off your tee-shirt. Very, very slowly. And then your bra, also very slowly. I want to look at every intimate inch of your glorious body before I begin to touch it.'

A shiver of wicked, exquisite anticipation ripped through her. She should have been back-pedalling; she wasn't. Being here was a step out of time and why shouldn't she just give in to this thing? She had always lived a life of responsibility. She had always toed the line, trundling along in the slow lane, while her sister had lived life to the full in the fast lane. She had spent so much time picking up the pieces of Jessica's misadventures that she was in serious danger of forgetting what being young and carefree was all about.

So why shouldn't she spend a few days out here remembering? She had a sudden craving for some misspent time before it was too late.

With a smile and then a gurgle of laughter, she hooked her fingers under her tee-shirt and did as he asked. She pulled it over her head very, very slowly. Then she reached back to unclasp her bra, which she also removed very, very slowly.

Then she gave Ryan a gentle push back and when he was lying on the sand she straddled him, her breasts like ripe fruit waiting to be handled.

Between her legs, his erection was a rod of steel pushing against her.

And the look in his eyes! The hunger and the appreciation.

'What else,' she asked wickedly, 'would you like me to do?'

RAMPANT appreciation flared in Jamie's eyes. She couldn't help it and, after days of blissfully throwing caution to the wind she no longer bothered trying to keep her guard up. Why should she? Ryan was nakedly, enthrallingly turned on by her. In their moments of wild passion, he would whisper how much into her ear, and every husky syllable represented yet another wrecking ball aimed at her defences.

And it wasn't just about the sex. They took time out, shooed out of the house by Vivian who claimed she needed peace and insisted that the only way she could get it was if they weren't making a racket in the house. Not that they did, but Ryan was happy to go with the flow. The island was stunningly beautiful and he had seen precious little of it. He hadn't realised how much of his work he took with him wherever he went, and for the first time he sidelined it in favour of showing Jamie around.

He took her to the Blue Hole where they swam in crystal clear waters. They took boats to the various islands. She forced him to traipse through bush so that they could experience some of the wildlife and laughed when he confessed to a fear of all things creepy-crawly.

'I think you'll find that *real* men, like me, are proud to admit to things like that,' he informed her haughtily, keeping a healthy distance as she allowed a praying mantis to scramble over her hand.

She had never had overseas holidays as a child. Losing her dad at such a young age had imposed financial restrictions on their lives. In the still, dark hours with just the sound of the sea lapping on the beach below the house, it seemed easy to shed her natural reserve and observe her childhood from a distance, with Ryan sitting next to her, an encouraging listener.

And of course they still worked together. Their mornings were still spent in the office in the house, but working had taken on a whole new perspective. They never touched one another, but sometimes he would lean over her, reading something over her shoulder on her computer, and his proximity was tantalising and electric. She would look at him and their eyes would tangle with full-blown lust even though they would be conversing perfectly normally about something mundane and technical.

Right now, Jamie was primly logging off her computer, but under her tee-shirt she was bra-less and under the small stretchy skirt the dampness between her legs announced the urgency her body felt at the prospect of being touched there.

Ryan was on the telephone, sprawled back in the leather swivel chair, his eyes broodingly following her movements as she stood up, smoothed down her skirt, caught his eyes and held them in a bold, inviting gaze.

'We got the contract.' He pushed back the chair, stuck his feet on the desk in a manner that was so typically him that it brought a half smile to her lips and beckoned her to him with his finger. 'George was eternally grateful for your exquisite attention to detail in the reports you emailed to him before the meetings began.'

'Good.' Jamie allowed herself a smile of professional satisfaction.

'Is that all you have to say by way of congratulations?' Ryan murmured, his eyes darkening as he took in the gentle sway of her breasts under the tight tee-shirt.

He was finding that he could barely look at her without his body slamming into immediate response. Where was the man with the formidable control when it came to women? He seemed to have been hijacked by a guy with a semi-permanent erection and a head full of erotic images that only went away when he was in deep sleep. Even then he had woken up on a couple of occasions to find himself thinking of her, needing an immediate cold shower, because despite his attempts at persuasion she had refused to share his bed for the duration of the night.

'What else would you like me to say?'

'I'm someone who believes that actions speak louder than words.'

'How would you like me to act?' Jamie blushed when he raised his eyebrows fractionally and let his eyes travel with slow, lazy insolence over the length of her body. 'We can't.' Her voice was breathless. 'Your mother will be waiting on the veranda for us to join her for lunch.'

'Forgot to tell you. She got Junior to drive her into town for a check-up with the consultant and she said that she's going to meet one of her friends for a bite out while she's there. I have yet, to see someone recover more quickly from a health scare,' he continued drily. 'In fact, I haven't seen her so relaxed in a long time.' Now that he and Jamie were open in their relationship, whatever that relationship might be, his mother was as chipper as a cricket, lapping it all up, planning who only knew what in that head of hers.

Ryan closed his mind to what lay round an otherwise unexplored corner in the future. Instead, he focused on the sexy, sexy woman standing inches away from him in a skirt that revealed newly brown, slender legs and a top that was begging to be ripped off.

'So you have all the time in the world to demonstrate how thrilled you are that we've managed to hook this new, lucrative contract. On second thoughts, I think that *I* should be the one to show *you* how impressed I am for your invaluable contribution to us closing the deal.'

He sat forward and ran his hands along the sides of her thighs, stroking their soft, silky length until he felt her begin to melt. Then he slid his hands higher, hooked his fingers over the lacy elastic of her underwear and tugged. Jamie trembled. She propped herself against the edge of his desk and closed her eyes, losing herself in the glorious sensation of skirt and panties both being pulled down. She was burning up even though the air-conditioning was on, circulating cold air through the room.

Their love-making was usually at night, after his mother had retired for the evening. The stars and the moon had borne witness countless times to them on the beach, lying on a giant rug on the sand, lost in each other. Twice they had cooled off in the sea only to fall right back into each other's arms the second they were out. They had made love in his bedroom. In her bedroom. Once, memorably, in the kitchen, late at night and with the kitchen door shut just in case, which had involved certain mouth-watering delights that Ryan had enjoyed licking off her.

But the office had been a designated work area so that now there was something deliciously wicked about being in it half-undressed.

'We should go upstairs,' she whispered. Her fingers sifted through his thick, dark hair. She looked down as he stared up at her for a few seconds.

'Oh, I don't know,' Ryan drawled. 'It seems only appropriate that I should show my deep and undying gratitude for your hard work in a working environment.'

'What if one of the gardeners sees us through the window?'

'Good point. I'll dip the shutters while you stay right where you are and don't move a muscle.'

She did and when he resumed his position on the chair she yielded to his devastating fingers and tongue until she was on the point of collapse. He tasted her until she thought that her whole body was going to explode, until she was begging him to take her. Her breasts ached under the tee-shirt and she was driven to roll her fingers over her sore, tender nipples in a bid to assuage their painful sensitivity. Every time she glanced down to that dark head buried between her thighs, she felt weaker than a rag doll. There was something intensely erotic about the fact that he was still fully clothed while she was dishevelled and half-dressed.

'I can't stand this any longer,' she groaned shakily, and she knew that he was smiling as he continued to tease her throbbing clitoris with his tongue.

'I love it when you say that.' Ryan finally released her screaming body from the onslaught of his attention and carried her, cave-man style, to the long sofa where she lay and watched as he stripped off his clothes. She never tired of feasting on the hard muscularity of his body.

Of course, he worked out. In London, he was a member of a gym, where twice a week he treated himself to gruelling games of squash with a couple of guys from the office. He also seemed to play every other sport imaginable. Here, he ran—at five in the morning, he had told her a few days ago. She hadn't believed him until this morning, on the way to the bathroom, she had glanced out of her window to see him disappearing down the drive. They had only gone their separate ways a few hours before. He was a man who needed next to no sleep.

When he lightly touched himself, an involuntary groan escaped her lips and he grinned. Her arm was resting lightly across her forehead and she looked like a very beautiful Victorian maiden caught in the act of swooning. Which, now that he thought about it, was an image that was intensely appealing.

'I'm glad you're satisfied with my level of appreciation, milady,' he told her huskily.

He positioned himself directly over her, her legs between his, and he pulled her tee-shirt over her head. She was already arching back, inviting his mouth to her breasts, offering the twin peaks of her nipples for his pleasure. Irresistible. Making love to her was a constant struggle to keep himself under control. The challenge of breathing in the dampness between her legs had been struggle enough when it came to self-restraint, and it was no easier as he dipped his head so that he could suckle on her nipples, one at a time, loving the way they engorged in his mouth.

He entered her with one single thrust when they could no longer bear to go so far but not far enough. Her body shuddered as within seconds she was climbing that peak, tumbling into an orgasm that rocked her body, taking him with her, their slick, slippery bodies fused as if one.

It was bliss to lie with him, squashed on the sofa, as they gradually came back down to earth. It was just as well that his mother was out, Jamie thought, because she knew that there was no way she could have sauntered out onto the veranda for lunch without betraying the tell-tale signs of a woman who has been branded thoroughly by her man.

She stretched, settled down more comfortably against his body. He cupped her breast absently, as though it was impossible for him to be this close to her without him touching her intimately. She loved it. She loved that feeling of possession. Sometimes he would cup between her legs or else just distractedly stroke her nipple with his finger, circling its outline and then teasing her as he waited for her to react to his feathery touch.

Jamie could have stayed like this for ever.

She said, reluctantly raising the subject, 'Now that the deal is done and dusted and your mother is pretty much back on her feet...'

Ryan stilled because he knew that this was a conversation they had to have. He was needed back in London. He could delegate, but only to a certain extent. Decisions had to be taken about crucial deals and those decisions could not be made out here where the tropical sun and gratifying, relaxing sex on tap—not to mention their daily jaunts out where thoughts of work disappeared—were combining to erode his appetite for ferocious concentration.

Jamie waited for him to pick up the threads of the conversation, but he didn't and she stifled a sigh.

'We should be thinking of returning to the UK.'

'Yes,' Ryan said slowly. 'We need to.' Until this moment, he had really not considered the matter in a truly concrete way. He did now. It took seconds. The truth, laid bare in front of him, was that he couldn't walk away from what they had begun. Had he envisaged this outcome when he had casually enrolled her in his clever plan to placate his mother's nervous concerns?

'I'll need to make reservations.'

'You know how to ruin an atmosphere, Jamie.'

'I'm not trying to. I'm just...being realistic.'

'We'll leave on the weekend. That's the day after tomorrow.' He rolled onto his back and stared up at the ceiling where the sun filtering through the half-open shutters played on the woodwork in an ever-changing kaleidoscopic pattern.

'And then we go back to being the people we were before we came here.'

'How easy is that going to be?' He inclined his head to look at her, but her face was giving nothing away. 'Do you really imagine that we're going to be able to return to the soulless working relationship we had before all of this?'

'It wasn't a soulless relationship!'

'You know exactly what I mean. We can't tell the past to go away because it's inconvenient.'

'What are you trying to say?'

'I'm saying that this stopped being a game of charades the second we climbed into bed, and if you think that we can pretend that none of it ever happened, then you're living in cloud cuckoo land. It happened, and it will still happen even when we're back in London and you're sitting at your desk and I'm at mine. When we look at one another, we're going to remember, and you can't wish that simple fact away.'

'We should never have started this.' There was always a price to be paid at the end of the day, and for so much pleasure the price was going to be steep. Jamie was now realising that she had got far more than she had bargained for. She had thrown off her old, careful, cautious self and let in a sentiment she now knew had been hovering on the sidelines, barely kept at bay, waiting to devour her. She had fallen in love with him and now she was drowning.

'Tell me I'm not going to get a long sermon loosely based on the notion of regret,' Ryan said curtly. 'I really thought that we had moved past all of that.'

'To what? Moved past it to what, exactly? You're right. It's going to be impossible to look at one another and pretend that none of this ever happened.'

'So we do the logical thing.' He smiled slowly and relaxed.

'Which is?'

'We continue seeing one another when we get back to London. What we have isn't going to go away because we tell it to, so why bother to try? If anyone had told me two months ago—less—that we would end up in bed together, and loving every second of the experience, I would have thought they were crazy. But here we are and I'm not willing to put this thing to sleep, not yet, not when I still burn for you and you're on my mind every second of the day.'

Not yet. Those two words stuck in Jamie's head and in between the glorious temptation to greedily take what was on offer the reality of its inevitable ending dripped through the fantasy like poison.

This was a moment in time, a moment which he wanted to extend because he was enjoying himself. He had broken through his self-imposed taboo of sleeping with someone he worked with, and now that he had done that it was all systems go as far as he was concerned.

He wouldn't be lying there, getting himself twisted into little knots, as he mentally journeyed into the future and found all the flaws in his plan. He wouldn't be stressing because at some indeterminate time their relationship would end and he would be left hurt and ripped to shreds. None of that would occur to him, because for him she was a casual fling, something that had defied belief in taking shape and, having taken shape, had further defied belief by being enjoyable. And Ryan Sheppard was a man with a very healthy capacity for enjoyment.

Looking at him now, he was the picture of a man satisfied with what he saw as a perfectly reasonable solution to a situation.

'I can't believe I'm saying this,' he confided, 'but you're the sexiest woman I've ever taken to my bed.' He folded her in his arms and covered her leg with his thigh. 'And, as an added bonus, you make me laugh.'

Jamie would have given anything to just close her eyes and carry on living for the moment, just as she had spent the past days doing. She had slept with him and loved every minute of it, but now they were about to head back to London, and she could no longer pretend that she was the kind of girl who could live indefinitely in the present without a thought of the future. She was cursed with the burden of responsibility and too well-trained in the many ways of dumping it on her shoulders.

'When I touch you,' he admitted roughly, 'I forget what the concept of stress is. I've never played truant until now—all those trips when the thought of work never crossed my mind. And my mother is overjoyed with this situation.' He kissed her eyelids, which fluttered shut. 'Let's not put a spanner in the works by talking about regret. We agreed to put on an act. We didn't have to, as it turns out. Let's see where this thing takes us, Jamie, and when it's over I won't have to concoct a lie to my mother.'

When it's over. She wondered how he could build so many negatives into something he was trying to persuade her was a positive step forward, but of course he wouldn't even be aware of that. He was so accustomed to the short-term nature of his relationships that he wasn't even capable of thinking of them in any other way. Every adjective he used reminded her that, for him, this was a sexually satisfying but temporary situation. How long would it take, once they had returned to London, before the sexiest woman he had ever taken to his bed became yesterday's news?

Here, on the island, there was no competition. In London, there would be competition lurking round every corner, waiting to ambush him from behind every door, phoning him and texting him and emailing him. Where would *she* stand then? He would no longer be playing truant and she wouldn't be the person making him laugh.

She pushed herself up into a sitting position, feeling suddenly very exposed without a stitch of clothing on.

'We should get up. Get dressed. I'm hungry, and your mother will be back soon. I'm sure she won't want to stay out for too long in this sun, not after what she's been through.'

'I doubt she would turn a hair if she discovered that we were doing more than filing reports in here.'

'That's not the point,' Jamie told him sharply. She began levering herself off the sofa, only to be pulled back down so that she half fell on top of him, her breasts squashing against his chest.

'This conversation isn't over,' he grated. 'You opened it, and neither of us is going anywhere until it's been closed.'

'I don't know what you want me to say.'

'You damn well do, Jamie.'

'Okay. You want me to tell you that I'll continue sleeping with you until you decide that you're sick of me and chuck me over for your usual blonde-haired, legs-up-to-armpits bimbo!'

'Where did *that* come from?' He pinned her to the sofa and stared at her fiercely, although underneath his bristling brows she could see his bewilderment. He hadn't a clue what had prompted that outburst and that, in itself, was hurtful. She had a brief, searing fantasy in which he soothed away her fears and insecurities by telling her that there would never be another blonde-haired, legs-up-to-armpits bimbo, that she was the only woman for him, that he worshipped the ground she walked on and loved her to death. The fantasy vanished virtually as soon as it materialised.

'I've really...enjoyed *this*, but when we get back to London, things between us are going to get back to what they were. I know it's going to be difficult, but it won't be impossible. You'll be busy and distracted with other deals in the pipeline. I'll be busy trying to get rid of my sister who is still at my house. Your mother will probably want to see you a bit more often than she has in the past. In no time at all, we'll both look back on this as if it was a dream, something that never really happened.'

Ryan couldn't quite believe that she was effectively dumping him. He knew that she had been a reluctant bed-partner. He knew that she had principles which, once upon a time, he would have derided as positively archaic but which he had come to respect. But once she had slept with him, he had assumed a straightforward path leading towards a mutually agreed-upon outcome. Hell, people embarked upon marriage with fewer scruples and less psychoanalysis! The thought of no longer being able to touch her—or, worse, of seeing her on a daily basis and no longer being able to touch her—made his blood run cold, but Ryan suddenly felt as though he had gone the extra mile in the seduction stakes. He wasn't going to beg.

'Besides, it would be awkward. Sooner or later, people would find out. You know how that office buzzes with gossip. Both of us would lose respect.'

'Do yourself a favour and don't worry on my behalf. Gossip has never bothered me.'

'Well, it would bother *me*,' Jamie told him coolly. 'I've never liked the thought of people talking about me behind my back. Anyway, let's be honest, this isn't a relationship that's going anywhere.' She was disgusted with herself for the tiny thread of hope that continued to blossom inside her, the hope that he would leap into instant denial or at least pretend to give the matter some serious thought.

But he just said with an impatient shrug, 'Why does a relationship have to go somewhere? We're happy with this. That's all that matters.'

'Not to me!'

'Are you telling me that you want me to ask you to marry

me?' Ryan said slowly, fixing her with those fabulous eyes
that gave the illusion of being able to see right down deep
into her innermost soul.

'No! Of course not!' Jamie gave a shaky laugh. In her
head, she could imagine his incredulity at such a preposter-
ous idea: the secretary who after a few days romping in the
sack suddenly got thoughts above her station, encouraged
by his mother. 'But I don't want to spend time with someone in a relationship that's not going anywhere. I guess I've
learnt some lessons from Greg.' Within reason, she was determined to be as truthful as possible.

'Right.' Ryan stood up and strolled towards the bundles
of discarded clothes on the floor, his back to her, offering
her a rejection that made her eyes sting. 'So it's back to business as usual,' he remarked, pulling on his clothes while she
continued to watch him helplessly. He found himself thinking of creative ways he could use to get her to change her
mind and scowled at his own weakness. He had had the rug
pulled from under his feet and that, he decided, was why he
now felt like hitting something very hard.

She had managed to scuttle back into her tee-shirt and
knickers by the time he eventually turned around.

'We could continue to enjoy ourselves for the little time
here we have left...' Jamie was ashamed of the desperation
behind this suggestion.

The fact that she was as cool as a cucumber enraged
Ryan even more. She had been nothing if not a star pupil,
he thought savagely. From shrinking violet, she was now
brazen enough to offer her body to him for a day and a half,
with their cut-off point doubtless to be when Junior was carrying their cases to the car.

'A few more sex sessions for the road?' he asked with
thick sarcasm and Jamie flinched. 'How many do you think
we can fit in before the car is revving in the drive to take us

to the airport?' This was supposed to have been fun. Once they returned to London, they would be working alongside one another and there would be no room for misplaced emotion.

Ryan shook his head, frustrated at his own inability to put things into perspective. Had it been a mistake to start this in the first place? Jamie was nothing like the women he had slept with in the past. At her core, she was intensely serious. She wasn't into the clubs, the parties and the expensive trinkets, and he had been challenged and seduced by the novelty of someone so different from what he was accustomed to. Add to the mixture the fact that she was intelligent and humorous, and then throw in the ease with which she had engaged his notoriously picky family members—was it any surprise that he had chosen to overlook the simple reality that she would not be satisfied with the sort of relationship he preferred?

'Get dressed.' He couldn't have a conversation with her when her body was still on tempting display.

Jamie went bright red and gathered up the rest of her clothing, taking his command for what it was. Now that they were over, he was already relegating her to his past. He was a guy who specialised in moving on when it came to women and he was already moving on, no longer interested in her body, possibly even turned off by the physical reminder of what they had shared.

She would take her cue from him. It had been a mistake to suggest that they enjoy themselves for the brief time they had left on the island, and she knew that that sign of weakness would return to haunt her at a later date.

'We'll have to maintain this fiction while we're still here,' Ryan told her with a shuttered expression and Jamie nodded, thankful for her hair swinging across her face as she looked down, hiding her giddy confusion.

She composed herself before raising her eyes to meet his. 'Of course.'

Her calm smile got on his nerves. He gritted his teeth together and shoved his hands into his pockets, where they bunched into fists.

'Look, I'm really sorry,' Jamie said awkwardly, trying to elicit a response, but the Ryan she had known over the past few days had disappeared from view. In his place was a cold-eyed stranger that chilled her to the bone and made her wonder whether they would ever be able to rescue their working relationship and return it to the uncomplicated place it had once inhabited.

'Sorry? For what?' He shrugged casually, walked towards the door and held it open for her to precede him out of the office, straight into the balmy tropical air that suddenly made him feel as though he was trapped in a greenhouse. 'I asked you to come here. You were quite happy to remain in London and play nursemaid to your sister.'

Jamie bit her lip and stifled the urge to argue with him on that point. He was now her boss once again and she seemed to have lost the right to speak her mind. Besides, he was barely aware of her presence, walking briskly towards the French doors and out onto the breezy veranda. She lagged behind and chose to hover by the door with her arms folded.

Ryan sprawled on one of the wicker chairs and stretched out his legs. 'I also persuaded you to play a role because it suited me, so I have no idea what you're sorry for, unless it's for climbing into bed with me—but, hell, we're both adults. We knew what we were signing up for.' He glanced over his shoulder to where she was dithering slightly behind him. 'Why don't you go and see to the arrangements for our flights back? And then you might as well use the rest of the day to get your things together.'

Jamie left him staring out at the distance. Effectively dismissed, she miserably obeyed orders. She managed to get them flights for the following day, which was a relief. In front of his mother, they made a passable show of togetherness but she retired very early for bed.

Landing in London was like reconnecting with a place she no longer recognised. After the sharp, bright technicolor of the island, and the slow, tranquil pace of life, the hustle and bustle of the grey streets and even greyer skies was a mournful reminder of what she had lost.

She felt like a different person—the person who had lived life in the slow lane, imagining herself to still have feelings for Greg, had disappeared. Ryan had awakened her and, for better or worse, she was no longer going to be the careful person in the background she had spent years cultivating.

For that, she was thankful. On every other score, the bright smile she kept pinned to her face bore no relation to the misery and confusion she was feeling inside—especially when, as they delivered Vivian to Claire and Hannah, both of whom had made the trip to the airport to collect their mother, she saw Ryan pick up a mobile on his cell phone.

She knew him so well that when he turned away, lowered his voice, gave that throaty chuckle, she realised that he was on the phone to a woman.

'Please tell me that I won't start back tomorrow with the usual delivery of flowers for the new woman in your life?' Her voice threatened to break when she said this, but it didn't, and in fact she was rather proud of her composure. The sun had turned him into a bronzed god and her breath caught in her throat as memories flooded her head, making her feel a little dizzy, but she kept smiling and smiling, even when he raised his eyebrows in a question.

'No idea what you're talking about.'

'Okay!' she said brightly, sticking out one hand to hail a cab.

'But if it did,' Ryan drawled, 'would it bother you?'

Jamie tugged her coat protectively around her. 'Honestly?'

Ryan felt an uninvited leap of interest. After the dance they had been doing around one another for the past day and a half, the thought of cutting through the facade was irresistible. A little honesty? Who could resist? He tilted his head to one side in a semi-nod.

'It wouldn't feel good.' Jamie kept her voice low, even and well-modulated. 'But I would do it, so please don't think that you would have to tiptoe around me. The working relationship we have is much more important to me than a brief fling. In fact...' She paused and glanced around her to where Ryan's driver was patiently waiting. He would be going straight to the office. She, on the other hand, would be returning to see what damage her sister had inflicted on her house in her absence.

'In fact...?' Ryan prompted.

'In fact, all said and done, you've done me a huge favour.'

'What are you talking about?'

'You've taken me out of cold storage. I think I had spent far too long kidding myself that I still had feelings for Greg. You made me see what a big mistake it was to bury myself in the past.' There was a strong element of truth in that but, more importantly, Jamie liked the control she could impose on her fractured life by rationalising her behaviour. She could almost kid herself that everything had happened for the best and, if she could convince herself of that, then she would be able to cope with Ryan whispering sweet nothings down the end of a phone to another woman. It made sense, and Jamie had to be sensible again. Her life depended on it.

'I'm a different person now. I'm going to really start enjoying London. I can see that I wasted a long time hibernating. Not consciously, of course, but I took a back seat and I shouldn't have. So, that's all I wanted to say. Except, well, your mother still thinks that we're about to tie the knot any second now... Can I ask you when you intend to tell her the truth?'

'Does it matter? After all, you're out of the equation now,' Ryan told her politely.

'Yes, but *what* will you tell her? I'm very fond of Vivian and the more I've got to know her the less I've liked what we did.'

'Don't worry. I won't blacken your name, Jamie.'

'Thank you, because I would quite like to see your family. Some time.'

'That won't be appropriate.'

'Right. I understand.' She felt a lump in her throat and looked away quickly.

'My mother is given to fond flights of fancy,' Ryan continued. 'And I don't want her to be encouraged into thinking that we're still an item. It won't work. As soon as she's settled back, I'll break the news to her that we've parted company, on perfectly amicable terms that allow us to carry on working harmoniously together. Rest assured that if my mother apportions blame to anyone, it'll be to me.'

'She'll be upset.' Jamie knew what it was like to live in a bubble and how painful it could be when that bubble burst.

'In which case, I shall have to make sure that I give her something else to think about and look forward to,' Ryan murmured, leaning down so that Jamie felt his warm breath against her ear, tickling her and doing all sorts of familiar things to her body.

'What do you mean?'

'Well.' He straightened up and shot her a devilish grin that made her toes curl. 'Maybe this has been a learning curve for both of us!'

'Really?'

'Of course! You haven't got the monopoly on life lessons, Jamie. Whilst you're busy getting out there and discovering London, let's just say that *I* might finally start my search for the perfect partner. My mother wants me to settle down. The harridans keep nagging me. Yes, maybe it's time for me to think about tying the knot!'

CHAPTER NINE

RYAN looked at the blonde perched on the sofa in his office and she looked expectantly back at him. She was in search of an evening of fun, involving a very expensive meal, a very expensive club and possibly a very expensive trinket to wear around that slender, white neck of hers, something that would complement the tumble of vanilla curls that fell to her waist in artful disarray.

It was Friday night and he couldn't think of a single reason why he shouldn't shove the work to one side and look forward to the prospect of what was prominently an offer.

Instead, he found himself thinking of excuses to back out of his evening of fun and he scowled at his own idiocy.

Where was Jamie? Ever since they had returned to London two weeks ago, she had turned into an annoying clock watcher. Only now did he realise how accustomed he had become to her willingness to work long hours at his beck and call, and only now did he realise how much of his time had been spent in her company. A Friday evening had often seen them brainstorming something, occasionally with some of his computer whizz-kids who could be relied upon to sacrifice entire weekends in the pursuit of tweaking computer programs, very often on their own, calling in a takeaway and enjoying it with files and papers spread between them on his desk.

Gone; all of it. She was still the super-efficient secretary, always polite and unfailingly professional, but now she left when she should leave and didn't arrive a second before she was due.

Clearly she was pursuing that fabulous single life she had mentioned when they had parted company at the airport. He wouldn't know. She never mentioned a word of it and there was no way that he was going to play the loser and actually show an interest.

Abigail, whom he had now seen a couple of times and of whom he was already beginning to tire, leaned forward, flashed him a coy smile and stood up.

'Are we actually going to go out, Ryan, baby? Please don't tell me that we're going to spend Friday night in this office!'

'I've spent many an enjoyable Friday night here,' Ryan grated, but standing up and moving to help her with her coat.

'Well.' She pouted and then stretched up to briefly peck him on the lips. 'That's not *my* sort of thing. And good luck finding any woman who would enjoy that!'

Which brought him right back to Jamie. Pretty much everything seemed to bring him right back to Jamie these days. He didn't want to feel driven to watch her, but he did. He absorbed the way she moved, the way she leaned forward when she was studying something in front of her, tucking her hair behind her ear and frowning. He absorbed the way she nestled the telephone against her shoulder when she spoke so that she could do something else at the same time and then the way she lightly massaged her neck afterwards. He noticed how she shifted her eyes away from him when he spoke to her, and the faint colour that stole into her cheeks, which was the only giveaway that under the polite surface all was not as evenly balanced as she would have him believe.

Or was it?

Ryan didn't know and he hated that. Having always found it easy to walk away from relationships once they had begun to out-stay their welcome, he was finding it impossible to do the same with this one. Why? He could only think that it was because what they had had been terminated before it had had time to run its course. It was unfinished business. How could he be expected to treat it with a sanguine shrug of the shoulders?

Also, *he* hadn't generated the break-up. Ryan knew that that was nothing but wounded male pride, but it went into the mix, didn't it? And the whole mix, for him, was adding up to a very unpleasant fixation which he was finding hellishly difficult to shift.

It would help if he could generate more of an interest in her replacement.

It was after ten by the time they entered the exclusive club in Knightsbridge. They had dined in one of the most expensive restaurants in London, where Abigail had made gentle digs about his choice of dress. He had ordered more wine to get him over his growing irritation. She had spent far too long trying to engage his attention on various titbits of gossip concerning friends he didn't know and could not care less about. She bored him with anecdotes about the world of acting, which made him recognise the folly of dating yet another woman who thought that everyone was interested in a bunch of people egotistic enough to imagine that what they did for a living really was of immense interest to the rest of the human race. Abigail tittered, trilled, pouted and flaunted a body that he considered far too thin, really.

The trip to the club would probably mark the death knell of the relationship, if relationship it could be called, and that was the only reason he entered with something approaching a spring in his step.

It took him a few seconds for his eyes to adjust to the dim lighting. The club was intimate, with a number of tables for anyone wanting to dine or just sit and enjoy the spectacle of people on the dance floor. The bar area, sleek and very modern, was busy and waiters were doing the rounds, taking orders and pocketing the very generous tips given by the patrons. A live jazz band ensured that the atmosphere remained up market and sophisticated.

Ryan had been to this club a number of times before but this time he was less than impressed by the subdued lighting and eye candy. Maybe he was getting too old for this sort of thing. He was in his thirties now and there was a fine line between trendy and sad. He hadn't seriously intended to start hunting for the perfect marriage partner, as he had nonchalantly told Jamie two weeks previously, but now he wondered whether the time really had come to settle down. After all, he didn't want still to be coming to this place in five years' time, with another Abigail clone hanging on to his arm.

On the verge of telling his date that if she wanted to stay she would be staying on her own, he spotted Jamie, and the shock of seeing his secretary in a *club* was almost enough to make him think that his eyes were playing tricks on him.

Since when did Jamie frequent clubs? Ryan was rocked by the upsurge of rage that filled him. Was this what she had been busily doing on all those evenings since they had returned to London, when she had tripped over herself to join the throng of people leaving the building on the dot of five-thirty? Was this her bid to throw herself into living life in the fast lane?

Abigail had spotted some of her friends and he absently nodded as she disappeared into the crowd by the bar. He was keen to see who Jamie had come with. Her sister, maybe? She hadn't told him the outcome of Jessica's situation. Obviously, that had been just too personal a conversation for her to endure, and pride had stopped him from asking.

However, Jessica must still be on the scene, perhaps having ditched the caring, sharing vet, and was now introducing Jamie to what she had been missing: a sleazy, over-priced night club in the heart of Knightsbridge.

Ryan almost laughed out loud. Had she come to him for advice on where to go, he would willingly have told her, and would have steered her away from the dubious pleasures of seedy joints where middle-aged men tried to pick up young girls.

He had three bottles of the finest champagne sent over to Abigail and her crowd of giggling friends and received a beaming smile of appreciation in return. Then he got himself a whisky and edged over to wait for Jamie. She had disappeared in the direction of the cloakroom, on her own. Several heads—he noticed grimly, several *male* heads—had followed her progress across the crowded room and he could understand why. Gone were the flat shoes, the hair neatly tied up, the sober suit. In fact, gone was everything he associated with his secretary. She had been at pains over the past couple of weeks to revert to projecting the hands-off image, a daily reminder of her position within his company and in his life. She worked for him. She obeyed orders. She carried out her duties. And she locked him out of everything else.

Ryan swallowed a generous slug of whisky and scowled. She had vanished temporarily but her image was still seared into his head: the high stilettos, the tight, outrageously short red dress, the poker-straight hair parted to one side so that it swept across her face, giving her a come-hither look that frankly set his teeth on edge.

He couldn't spot Jessica anywhere or else he would have been tempted to personally congratulate her on the miraculous transformation of her sister.

He had worked his way towards the door through which Jamie would return and was on his second whisky by the time she emerged. He was in just the right position to reach out and grab her by the arm.

It gave her the fright of her life.

Jamie was bitterly regretting the crazy impulse that had brought her to the club with Richard, one of Greg's friends to whom she had been introduced just three days previously. Clubs just weren't her thing. The music seemed very loud, too loud to permit any sort of decent conversation, and it was really dark—especially when wearing very high heels. One wrong move and she would embarrass herself by crashing to the floor, so she had spent the past two hours taking very small steps and only reluctantly allowing herself to be dragged to the dance floor for a couple of upbeat tunes that she recognised.

And Richard... Well, he was a nice enough guy, fashioned in the same mould as Greg. Both of them had been to university together and both had studied to be vets, with Richard opting to work in London while Greg had moved north. He should have made the ideal date and Jamie was sure that, had she met Richard a year before, she would have warmed to his gentle personality and perhaps even embarked on a relationship that might have gone somewhere.

But she had been ruined by Ryan. Her ideal man no longer seemed to be the kind, placid sort. Compared to Ryan, with his vibrant, explosive, overpowering personality, Richard was a shadow of a man and they had established early on that there was no attraction. Which made this excursion to the club slightly more bearable; at least she didn't have to ward off unwanted attention from her date.

But she had dressed to kill and she knew that other men had been looking at her.

She was half-expecting one of them to sidle over and really throw her into a tizzy by asking her to dance, and the sudden tug on her arm as she emerged from the cloakroom where she had been taking cover for as long as had been humanly possible made her jackknife in startled horror.

Jamie turned, mouth open, to give whoever had had the nerve to grab her a piece of her mind. She was also poised to run. The club seemed full of lecherous old men with suspiciously young and beautiful girls dangling like trophies on their arms.

She was so taken aback at seeing Ryan that her mouth literally fell open in startled shock.

'What are *you* doing here?'

'Snap! I was about to ask *you* the same thing. Are you here with your sister? Painting the town red?'

'No, I'm not. And, in fact, I'd better get back to my table. My date will be wondering where I am.'

'Date? Date? What date? Are you telling me that you're here with a *man*?'

Jamie bristled at the tone of his voice. Did he imagine that she was incapable of having a life outside work? She had made it perfectly clear that she did. She had been at pains over the past fortnight to make sure that she left on time and arrived on time, the implication being that she had lots of other exciting things to do with her life aside from devoting all her time to him.

'That would be most people's definition of a date!'

'You came here with him or did you pick him up here? Because if you picked him up here then I would have to warn you to lower your expectations. Most of these guys come here to scout and see what they can pick up.'

Jamie started moving away and Ryan followed her. She had come here with a man. He was outraged at the thought of that. It felt suddenly imperative that he meet this guy. How had she managed to achieve that in the space of two weeks? Of course, he knew how. She had the body of a siren and she had obviously been determined to flaunt it.

His jaw tightened, and he was further disgruntled to discover that the man rising to greet her looked like a decent sort of guy: short brown hair, pleasant smile, wire-rimmed spectacles. Just the sort of man she had once professed to go for. Ryan tried not to scowl as introductions were grudgingly made. She hadn't been aware of him following her but, having turned around to see him towering behind her, she had had no option but to introduce the men to each other.

Next to Ryan, Richard looked flimsy and insubstantial, which further annoyed her.

'Can I be terribly rude, old man—' Ryan stepped in before she could dismiss him, which was what she clearly had in mind '—and ask your date for a dance? She left work ridiculously early today.'

'I left on time!'

'And there were one or two things I needed to discuss with her. I don't normally drag my work out with me, but...'

'Aren't you here with someone?' Jamie asked tartly, then she lowered her voice to hiss into his hear. 'Or are you one of those men who come here scouting to see what they can pick up?'

'Not my style.' He slipped his arm around her waist, already taking it as a given that the neat little guy she had come with would give his permission to have his date whipped away for a few minutes. He didn't look like the sort to put up much of a fight. Indeed, the man was happy to let his hot, sexy date get on the dance floor with someone else's arms wrapped around her, even though the hot, sexy date was making all sorts of noises about feeling tired and needing to sit it out.

'Tired?' Ryan murmured in a low, velvety drawl that had her skin breaking out in goose bumps. 'Surely not? How are you going to paint any town red if you're yawning at eleven on a Friday evening?'

The music had obligingly shifted from fast to slow, and Jamie stiffened as he pulled her towards him in a clinch that was far too intimate for her liking. She tried to pull back and he tugged her closer, resting his hand on the small of her back, reminding her of what it felt like to be touched by him. It was not a memory she wanted to linger over.

'I'm sure your date wouldn't approve of us dancing,' she said primly, following his lead and trying to hold herself as rigidly as possible. 'Where is she, anyway?'

'Behind you—a quarter to ten. Bright blue dress. Blue shoes.' He swung her around so that Jamie had a perfect view of a tall blonde with lots of long, tousled blonde hair and long, long legs. The pull of jealousy was so overpowering that she felt momentarily giddy.

Ryan had kept this one quiet. There had been no emails popping up on his computer, the password for which Jamie had, no breathy phone calls, no mention of anything having to be rearranged so that he could fit in his latest woman.

She didn't want to think about it, but she did. Was this one the serious one?

'She's very pretty,' Jamie said crisply. 'Have you introduced her to your mother as yet?'

'My mother,' he said into her ear, dipping her which made her feel very exposed in her too revealing dress, 'has yet to learn that you and I have broken up.'

'You mean you haven't told her?'

'No opportunity. Who's the guy, Jamie? Now that you've quizzed me about my date.'

'I haven't quizzed you!'

'Are you trying to avoid my question?' Her breasts against his chest were turning him on and he drew back slightly rather than risk having her feel his erection pushing against his zip.

'I don't see that it's any of your business.'

'I'm concerned about you. We *were* almost married, don't forget.'

'We were *never* almost married!'

'My mother would probably disagree. So I don't feel it's out of place to tell you that it's a big, bad world out there and you don't have much experience of it. In the space of a couple of weeks, you've managed to get yourself a man. He could be anybody.'

'How dare you?' Jamie gritted. 'I don't believe I'm hearing this!'

'You should be flattered that I continue to take an interest in your welfare. That guy may have a neat haircut and wear deodorant but it doesn't necessarily make him one of the good guys.'

Jamie almost snorted in disgust. Did Ryan Sheppard consider *himself* one of the good guys? Good guys didn't string women along! She bit back the temptation to ask him whether his date for the night—the one who had been abandoned in favour of his secretary for no other reason than he was incurably *nosy*—would categorise him as a 'good guy' when she was probably after love, marriage and the whole fairy-tale story. Chances were slim that he would deliver.

In fact, she wanted to ask him just how serious he was about the blonde. But there was no way that she was going to do that. The past two weeks had been agonising. Every day had been a challenge to not look at him, not react to him, desperately try to pretend that she was over whatever passing fling they had enjoyed. She wasn't going to encourage any kind of personal conversation now, and it infuriated her that just being here with him, seething at everything he had just said, still made her feel more alive than she had felt ever since she had returned to London.

'You read the papers. You watch the news. Low lifes are everywhere and some of them do a good job of passing for normal.'

'Well, thank you very much for you concern and your wise words, Ryan, but you can relax. Richard comes with personal recommendations.'

'Really? Spill the beans.'

'Greg introduced me to him, if you must know. He and Greg went to university together and Richard works in London.'

'Another vet? Didn't you get your fill of guys who miss their sickly animals whenever they're away from them for too long?'

'I'm not going to stand here and listen to this.'

'You're not standing. You're dancing.' He twirled her around and watched as the colour mounted in her cheeks and her hair became tangled and dishevelled. 'And is vet-number-one here with his erstwhile wife?'

The music stopped but when Jamie would have walked off he kept her firmly anchored by virtue of his fingers curled around her wrist. Out of the corner of his eye, he could see Abigail looking at them with scowling displeasure, and he knew that he should go across to her, at least make a show of wanting to spend some time in her company.

Without releasing Jamie, he beckoned across a waiter, who magically materialised, and whispered something into his ear. A few more bottles of champagne, he reasoned, to be delivered to the tall blonde in the blue dress—and his most sincere apologies, but he had business to discuss with his secretary. The thought of abandoning his conversation with Jamie was out of the question.

'I'm sure your date won't mind if we trip the light fantastic for a bit longer. And you were going to tell me about Vet One and your sister.'

Jamie gave an exasperated sigh. She didn't want this. She didn't want to be dancing with him, to feel his hand resting on her waist and the heat from his body scorching her. She was aware of the guilty thrill spreading through her body and she didn't want that either. She reasoned that it would do no good to storm off in a petulant strop. She was only dancing with him, for heaven's sake! And, besides, Ryan could be as tenacious as a dog with a bone. Did she really want him following her to her table? Joining them? Calling across his girlfriend to share the fun and laughter? No! One more dance and he would be gone and she would be able to breathe properly, she told herself fiercely.

'They've patched things up,' she said reluctantly and Ryan held her back so that he could look at her with interest.

'Why haven't you told me this before?'

'I didn't think that you would be that interested.'

'I'm cut to the quick, Jamie.' His voice was light, but he was surprised to discover that he didn't like being kept out of the loop with this information. Hell, she had retreated back into her impenetrable fortress and slammed the door firmly in his face. 'What happened?'

'Long story.'

'I'm happy to keep dancing until you've got it off your chest.'

'I had a heart-to-heart with Jessica when I got back to London.' Jamie was distracted enough not to notice the way he had pulled her closer to him. She thought back to that fateful conversation with her sister. It had been the best thing she had ever done and for that, she knew, she owed a great deal of thanks to Ryan and his family. She had seen, first hand, how relationships between family members should operate. She had witnessed how important it was to be open and honest.

She had also not been in the best of moods, back in her house, when she had been confronted with a sister who had not budged in her stance that marriage was a bore and she was due a life of fun and excitement. Greg was still there trying to play the persuasive card and so, it seemed, were all the ensuing arguments.

For the first time in both their lives, Jamie had sat her sister down and really given her a piece of her mind.

'I told her that it wasn't acceptable for her to descend on me and not really give a hoot whether she was disrupting my life or not. I told her that she was thoughtless and inconsiderate and that she was old enough to sort out her problems. I also said that she was being an utter fool, that Greg was crazy about her, that he was a treasure, and that if she decided to end the relationship then she should do it and stop dithering. Most of all I told her that she would have to sort things out somewhere else because I was fed up with both of them in the house.'

'A red-letter day for you, in other words,' Ryan murmured. Wisps of her hair brushed his lips and he stifled a shudder of pure craving. When she looked up at him with an open, genuine smile, the first he had glimpsed since they had returned to London, he was overwhelmed with the crazy sensation of just not feeling right in his own skin.

'It all came out then. Jessica told me that she was terrified of getting pregnant and losing her figure. I suppose I always envied her. She did what she wanted to do, and she always pulled it off because she was so beautiful, while I stayed in the slow lane, always being responsible, always there to pick up the pieces.'

Talking to him, Jamie realised how much she had missed it. It was unbelievable that in such a short period of time she had become accustomed to sharing her thoughts with him and appreciating his always humorous, always intelligent take on whatever she had had to say.

She felt a suspicious lump at the back of her throat and looked away quickly. It was very important not to give in to all those waves of nostalgia and regret that had a nasty habit of sneaking up on her when she wasn't looking. She had to remember that they had moved on from that place of lovers. He had a new girlfriend—probably a model or an actress, by the looks of her—thereby proving that he would always run true to form, that *she* had been nothing but a novelty to be enjoyed on the run. And she, in turn, had been making a huge effort to get out there. Well, she had accepted a date, which was a promising start.

'So there you have it!' she told him brightly. 'Not a particularly interesting story.'

'Let me be the judge of that. So where was hubby when all this soul-searching was taking place?'

'Out meeting Richard for a drink.'

'How very thoughtful of him to introduce the two of you.'

Jamie was finding it hard to recall exactly what Richard looked like. As usual, Ryan's image superimposed itself on everything and she felt angry and helpless at the same time at his way of just taking over her thoughts.

'Yes. We hit if off instantly.'

'Did you, now?' Ryan said through gritted teeth.

'Maybe I have a thing for vets!' she trilled gaily. 'Just like you have a thing for actresses and models.' Jamie hadn't wanted to say that, but the words popped out of her mouth, and her heart sank a little when he didn't utter a blanket denial to her sweeping generalisation.

'Maybe you do. Well, make sure that you give me ample warning if you decide to get married and start having a brood of children.'

'I don't think that marriage is something to be rushed into. Besides, I've only been out with Richard...' *once* '...a couple of times.' She smiled politely and drew away from him as the song came to an end. 'And, yes, I'll make sure that I tell you well in advance if and when I decide to tie the knot.'

'Hell, Jamie, have you ever heard of playing the field?' Ryan raked his fingers through his hair and glowered at her. A couple of dates and she wasn't denying the possibility that this might be the real thing! He wanted to root her to the spot, involve her in another dance, take the opportunity to tell her that throwing herself into the first relationship that came her way so shortly after they had broken up wasn't the right thing to do, but she was already walking away, threading a path through the crowds.

'You know that's not the way I am!' she told him over her shoulder, her voice bright and casual. 'And please don't follow me back to the table or I shall begin to feel really guilty about your poor girlfriend having to amuse herself.'

'Abigail's perfectly fine.'

'Really? Because she seems to be seething.'

'Question.'

Jamie stopped and looked at him. Even in this crowded place, he dominated his surroundings. His physical beauty leapt out and made a nonsense of all the other men in the cavernous room. No wonder his girlfriend looked put out. The competition in the club was stiff, lots of airhead blondes with long legs and short skirts, and a fair amount of them were openly sizing up the biggest fish in their midst.

'What is it?'

'Have you slept with him yet?'

His light-hearted, bantering tone said it all and an angry flush spread across her cheeks. Was he laughing at her? Was he thinking that she cut a ridiculous figure here, out of her comfort zone, dressed like a bird of paradise but without the streaming long hair and the endless legs? She wanted to hit him, and she balled her hands into fists and narrowed her eyes coldly.

'I really think it's time we ended this conversation, Ryan. I'll see you at work on Monday. Have a good weekend.' She turned away abruptly and walked with quickened strides towards the table, where Richard was waiting for her.

Why, she agonised, couldn't she have fallen for a man like Richard Dent? On paper, he was everything she had always reckoned she would want in a prospective partner. He was pleasant to look at, he was friendly, considerate and thoughtful. He had brought her flowers and had ruefully but manfully accepted it when she had told him that she liked him as a friend but that she wasn't interested in promoting a relationship with him. They had talked and, when she might have expected him to make his excuses and leave as soon as he could, he had insisted that they go out to the club, because why shouldn't friends have fun together?

She tried very hard to focus on what he was saying but her eyes kept straying, searching out Ryan, watching his body language with his girlfriend, torturing herself with thoughts of what they would be getting up to later.

Jamie spotted them leaving when Richard dragged her up to the dance floor for one last dance. Ryan's girlfriend seemed to be doing a great deal of excited gesticulating. He appeared to be ignoring her. Before she could look away, he caught her gaze, held it and then gave a slight inclination of his head. To her it seemed like a mocking salute, and in response she unconsciously and defensively allowed herself to relax in Richard's arms.

Of course it was a foolish, hollow gesture. Whilst he would be heading back to his place to fall into bed with yet another pouting blonde, she would be giving Richard a light embrace, exchanging mobile numbers and promising to meet up for a drink when their diaries permitted.

Her house, when she returned an hour later, seemed eerily empty. Jessica had taken everything with her and once Jamie had cleaned the place it was as though her sister had never been there. They had parted on good terms, and for the first time she wished she had her sister with her, someone to talk to instead of wandering alone into the kitchen where she made herself a cup of coffee and settled down to consider her options.

The reality of seeing Ryan with another woman had come as a brutal shock. Ahead of her stretched an endless future of seeing him with other women, waiting for him to fall in love with one of them. Out there, there would surely be a leggy blonde who had the personality to suck him in. How would she feel when that happened? Would she still be able to plaster a professional smile on her face and pretend that everything was all right? And, if she honestly couldn't see that happening, then surely the only course of action left would be to hand in her resignation?

It seemed like the next step forward and she was doodling on a piece of paper, working out what she would write, how she would explain her defection from a highly paid job which she had always loved, when the doorbell rang.

Jamie could only think that it might be Richard, at nearly one-thirty in the morning.

Still in her small red dress, but with her shoes kicked off in favour of some fluffy bedroom slippers, she wearily pulled open the door to find Ryan lounging outside, hands in his pockets.

'Do you usually open your door at this hour of the morning to anyone who comes calling?' He looked past her, compelled to see whether there was evidence of her date lurking around. 'It's dangerous.' He placed the flat of his hand on the door. 'You're going to ask me what I'm doing here and then you're going to tell me to leave. I'm not leaving. I want to talk to you. No—I *need* to talk to you. Where is your date?'

'He dropped me home and then left.' She hesitated, then took a deep breath. 'Which is just as well, because I need to talk to you too.' In that moment, Jamie made her mind up. She would have to hand in her resignation. She couldn't have Ryan taking time out from his hectic love life to deliver unwanted, uninvited advice to her. She didn't want him preaching to her about things she should or shouldn't do because they had been lovers and therefore he felt a misplaced sense of obligation. She certainly didn't want him thinking that he had a right to show up at her house whenever he felt like it to sermonise about her choices.

She led the way towards the kitchen and made him a mug of black coffee. Then she swivelled the draft copy of her resignation letter towards him.

Ryan stared down at it for a few seconds, during which his brain seemed to grind to a standstill. He picked up the piece of paper and reread her few polite lines but nothing appeared to be sinking in. 'What's this?'

'What does it look like, Ryan? It's my letter of resignation.' She wrapped her hands around the mug and stared at him, her heart racing like someone caught up in a panic attack. 'It's just a draft. I intend to type it out properly and it'll be on your desk first thing on Monday morning.'

'Over my dead body.' He crumpled the letter and tossed it on the table. 'Resignation not accepted!' He stood up, walked across to her, leaned down and shot her a look of savage fury. 'You're not resigning, and you're definitely not going to waste your time with that loser you're dating.'

CHAPTER TEN

'Don't you dare tell me what to do, Ryan Sheppard!' Jamie cringed back in the chair.

'Somebody's got to. For your own good.'

'Is that why you dashed over here? To give me a long lecture on being careful, because I'm obviously too naive and simple-minded to actually know how to live my own life?'

'You can't be serious about that guy after a couple of dates.' He pushed himself away from her and prowled angrily through the small kitchen, his movements jerky and restless. 'Did you tell him about us? Did he ask you to leave your job because of it? Because if that's the case then I'm warning you that the man is no good for you. Can you really see yourself in a position of subservience for the rest of your life?'

Jamie looked at him in complete bewilderment.

'Have you been drinking?' she asked eventually, which earned her a glowering look.

'You would drive any sane man to drink,' Ryan muttered under his breath. 'You told me that marriage wasn't on the cards!'

'Are you *jealous*?'

'Should I be?'

The silence stretched between them. 'Have you done anything that I should be jealous about?' Ryan shook his head and dealt her an accusing look. 'I don't do jealousy. I never have.' Suddenly those standard words which had once been true were exposed for the lie that they were. He was jealous as hell. Wasn't that why he had rushed over to her house? The thought of her being touched by anyone else had galvanised him into frantic action. She was still in her clubbing clothes. Had her date touched her underneath the skimpy little red dress?

Had he just missed the man by a whisker? Suddenly Ryan felt as though he needed something a lot stronger than a mug of black coffee.

'You can't resign,' he said finally. 'I won't let you.'

'Is that because I'm so indispensable? No one's indispensable. I think I'm quoting you when I say that. I can work out my month's notice and I'll make sure that I find someone equally dedicated to replace me.'

'You're irreplaceable.'

Jamie ignored the flush of pleasure those words gave her. Of course, Ryan would think her irreplaceable. Not only was he accustomed to the way she worked, but now that he had slept with her he must truly have entered his comfort zone. The physical side of their relationship might be over, but at the back of his mind he would always have how submissive and responsive she had been with him. It would have been easy for him to assume that that responsiveness would have been lasting, that she would have been even more obliging when it came to working overtime and putting herself out to suit him. Hence his horror now, faced with her resignation.

'Oh, please,' Jamie retorted with biting sarcasm.

'I didn't like seeing you with that guy.'

Jamie was so busy stoking herself into self-righteous anger, that Ryan had had the nerve to invade her privacy so that he could lecture her, that it took a few seconds for those words to sink in.

'What do you mean?'

'It seems that I do get jealous after all,' Ryan muttered in such a low voice that Jamie had to strain her ears to hear what he had said.

He returned to sit at the kitchen table, where he proceeded to frown at the floor before leaning forward, elbows on his thighs, rubbing his eyes with his fingers then looking up at her.

'You're jealous…' Jamie's heart sang.

'You've disappeared every evening on the dot of five-thirty ever since we got back to London.' Ryan glared at her accusingly. 'And then suddenly I discover the reason why. You've been going to clubs and seeing men behind my back.'

'I haven't been *seeing men*, and anyway you've been seeing women as well,' Jamie countered, without letting on that she had been torn apart with her own little green monsters. And had he told her anything about his latest blonde? No, he had been spectacularly silent on that matter, so how dare he start criticising her for trying to have a life?

'Abigail was a mistake. I have no idea what I was thinking.'

'Did you…did you sleep with her? Not that I care. I'm just curious.'

'You *should* care. You should care about everything I say and do and think because that's how I feel about you. And, no, I didn't sleep with her. I wasn't even tempted.'

Jamie breathed in sharply, almost not wanting to exhale just in case she broke the spell. Had he just said what she thought he had, or was she just imagining it?

'You didn't even tell me about your sister.'

'I…I was scared to carry on confiding in you, Ryan. I felt that we had been down that road and that if we were to con-

tinue working together then things would have to go back
to where they had once been. I would have to start learning
how to keep my private life to myself.'

'I was cut out of the loop and I didn't like it,' Ryan told
her heavily.

Jamie felt giddy when their eyes met. Her mouth was
dry and suddenly the kitchen just wasn't the right place to
be having this kind of conversation. Her thoughts were in a
muddle and she was beginning to ache from the hard kitchen
chair. She needed to sink into something soft and yielding
that would mould her trembling body.

'Perhaps we should go into the sitting room,' she suggested in a shaky voice. 'And if you're finished with that
coffee I can make you another.'

'Because you think I need to sober up? I've had a bit to
drink, but I'm by no means drunk.'

Jamie didn't say anything. She walked into the sitting
room, very conscious of him following behind her. She had
no idea what to make of what he had said to her. He was
jealous; he *cared* about what she thought. He stridently, ag-
gressively and possessively wanted her to care about what
he thought. And he hadn't slept with the blonde bombshell.

Every instinct in her was nourishing the fragile shoot of
hope that had begun to grow, but experience was still holding fast. She had made mistakes in the past. She forced herself to remember Greg. In retrospect, he had been nothing,
but at the time she had happily built castles in the air and
started hoping.

And then, with Ryan, she had fallen for him and had kid-
ded herself that hopping into bed with him had been a moment of complete recklessness that she had long deserved.
She had blinded herself to the obvious, which was that she
had more than wanted him. She had needed him, was depen-
dent and addicted to him. Then, once they had slept together,

she had immersed herself in the pretence of being involved for Vivian's benefit, and those important lines between reality and fantasy had become blurred. She had started hoping for things. She seemed to make a habit of it.

So now, although she was badly tempted to take everything he said at face value and put the best possible interpretation on it, she resisted. Where would it get her? Was he just after a few more weeks or months with her because the leggy blondes were not quite doing it for him at this point in time? Or was he interested in having her around because he had chickened out of telling his mother the truth and he wanted to buy a little more time before he broke the news to her?

'I don't understand why you're telling me all of this now,' she said as soon as she was on the sofa. 'If you cared so much about being out of the loop, then it's funny that you didn't show any interest for the past couple of weeks.' She looked at him levelly. He had taken up position on one of the squashy chairs. It allowed her important breathing space. Still, she knew that her body was alive with emotion. Like an illness, the symptoms of which were branded in her brain, she could recognise all the familiar responses he evoked in her.

'You dumped me, Jamie.'

'I had to.' She looked away quickly, her face colouring. 'I'm not casual enough for a prolonged fling. I told you that at the time and I meant it.'

'Which brings us back to the date. Has he made you promises you think he'll keep?'

Jamie sighed and shook her head. 'It was nothing serious,' she confessed. 'Richard is a really nice guy, but…' *But he's not you.* 'But maybe I don't go for vets after all.'

'And I don't go for leggy blondes, now that we're on the confession bandwagon. It doesn't matter what glossy magazine they've stepped out of.'

Jamie held her breath, then exhaled slowly. 'What do you mean?' She watched cautiously as he stood up and walked towards her, hesitating before sitting down on the sofa.

'I used to, once. A hundred years ago. I thought it was what I wanted—a rich, rewarding work life and fun on the side with women who didn't make demands. I don't know when things started to change,' Ryan admitted with painful honesty. 'You came to work for me, Jamie, and you spoilt everything I had always taken for granted.'

'What do you mean?' But the open vulnerability on his face made her heart swell. When he reached out to stroke her wrist, she didn't pull her hand away.

'I got accustomed to having a relationship with a woman on my own level.'

'We didn't *have* a relationship.'

'I'm not talking about a sexual relationship. I'm talking about an emotional and intellectual relationship. Those are the strongest building blocks on the face of the earth, only I didn't realise it at the time. I just knew that I was increasingly frustrated with the women I dated. They were empty and shallow and they bored me. And then we went away, and we didn't just sleep together. We…we talked.

'For the first time this week, it finally dawned on me just how much time we spent together, how much I enjoyed that and just how far down the road I'd gone when it came to really having a conversation with a woman. When it was gone, it was like something I should have appreciated and valued had disappeared from my life and I didn't know how to reclaim it. We got back to London and you were never around. I missed you. I miss you.'

'You miss me?' Jamie stretched those three words out for as long as she could, so that she could savour every syllable.

'When you kissed me at that Christmas party, it was as if a light had suddenly started shining from nowhere. I told myself that you had only kissed me to make the vet jealous. I figured that you were still emotionally wrapped up with him.'

'I stopped being wrapped up with Greg a long time ago. He started going out with my sister, and I can't even remember being terribly upset about it, although I thought that I *should* be.' That episode was like a dream she had had a million years ago. It was something that was no longer relevant in her life at all. 'I kissed you because my sister was going to. She'd had too much to drink. I wasn't about to let Greg see his wife kissing some other guy under a sprig of mistletoe. That would have been the end of their marriage and there was no way I was going to allow that to happen.'

'And that's the only reason why?'

Jamie went bright red.

'I've bared my soul,' Ryan murmured. 'Are you going to shoot me down in flames now by not being truthful with me? I can take it.'

'I kissed you because I wanted to.' She met his eyes, held them. 'I didn't think so at the time but, looking back on it afterwards, yes, I wanted to kiss you because I'd been attracted to you practically from the first time I set eyes on you, Ryan Sheppard.'

'But you once told me that attraction wasn't enough.'

Her breath caught in her throat. They had both said a lot to each other, but the word 'love' had never entered the conversation. She had never allowed herself to wear her heart on her sleeve and even now it floated unspoken around them, challenging either one to pluck it out of the silence and give it a name. When Jamie thought about doing that, her throat went dry and she felt as though she suddenly had cotton wool stuffed in her mouth.

'I remember,' she croaked shakily.

'You were right.' He fiddled with her fingers but Jamie

could hardly concentrate on that. 'I fell in love with you and I don't even know when it happened. When we finally made love, I never stopped to ask myself why it just felt so damned *right*.'

'You fell in love with me?'

'You look shocked,' he said wryly. 'I'm surprised you haven't put two and two together already. I said goodbye to Abigail and couldn't wait to get over here. I was going mad wondering what you were getting up to with your date. He looked like the kind of sensitive, tree-hugging guy who wouldn't hesitate to pour out his feelings after five seconds. I felt like I'd left things too late.'

'I can't believe you love me.' Jamie reached out one tremulous hand to stroke his cheek. 'I love you too. I feel like I've waited all my life for you. When we made love and got involved in that pretend relationship for your mother, I knew that I couldn't carry on with it when we got back here because I would want much more. I knew you were into flings, and I knew that if you tossed me aside I would never recover. I thought that I had to be proactive.'

Ryan pulled her into him. After two weeks, the feel of her body against his was like a taste of coming home.

They fell back onto the sofa and she wriggled on top of him. It was unbelievably good. When he began kissing her, she was completely lost.

Later, she struggled to remember how they had made it up to her bedroom. She had a fuzzy recollection of clothes being discarded along the way.

She gave herself to him with a blissful sense of completion. There was no other way of describing it—Ryan Sheppard *completed* her. Without him, she was lacking.

Afterwards, with his arms around her, he murmured softly into her hair, 'Now, my darling, I never want to go through the torture I've been through over the past few weeks. I'm afraid your brief taste of clubbing is at an end, unless I'm there, keeping a watchful eye on you. And the only way I can think of doing that is to marry you. So...will you marry me, Jamie?'

'Yes!'

'As soon as possible?'

'Absolutely!'

'I'm a happy man.' He lay back, one arm flung over the side of the bed, and smiled with contentment as Jamie covered him with little kisses.

Left to his own devices, Ryan would have married Jamie within the week. His mother, however, was having nothing of the sort. She wanted a full-blown affair, and in spite of his low-level grumbling—for he couldn't understand why on earth she hadn't already had her fill of full-blown weddings with his three sisters—Jamie was thrilled to accommodate her.

She was even more thrilled when Jessica offered to come down to London for a week so that they could go bridal shopping together.

'But no clubs and drinking,' Jamie felt compelled to warn her sister the week before she was due to arrive, and her warning was met with a burst of laughter.

'You have my word,' Jessica readily agreed. 'I'm pregnant! I was going to wait and surprise you with a picture of the scan, but I might just as well tell you over the phone. So when we're not looking for the perfect ivory wedding dress you might find yourself checking out prams and cots.'

Jessica had changed in more ways than one. Having confessed to feelings of deep insecurity at the thought of losing her figure should she get pregnant, she had finally surfaced to realise that Greg loved her for the person she was and not for the perfect figure she happened to have had imprinted in her genetic code.

And, as Jessica always did, she was now throwing herself into her pregnancy, even travelling with her baby books which she insisted Jamie read.

'Because you'll be next...'

It proved to be an accurate prediction.

One year and two months later, Jamie would sit in Ryan's apartment with a dark-haired, gloriously chubby-faced Isobella gurgling in her basket next to her and with details of country properties spread out on the table.

'London,' Ryan had announced, 'is no place to bring up a baby. At least, not central London.'

So they were moving out to Richmond. Not too far, but far enough from the traffic and chaos. As was Ryan's style, once the decision had been made he moved into immediate action, sourcing houses and submerging himself so well into the role of the domesticated man that Jamie could only sit back and smile.

Loving her, he had told her, had changed him. The birth of his first child had changed him even more. Gone was the workaholic and in its place was a man who enjoyed immersing himself in all the small things that made life go round.

Now Jamie joined him in the kitchen, where he was pouring them both a glass of wine, and she dangled a brochure in front of her.

'Not too big,' she said, 'not too small and in the perfect location...'

'I knew that one would get to you.' He dropped a kiss on her head and grinned. 'Clambering roses, beams, view of the park... We'll have to wait and see, though. As we both know, size matters.'

Jamie giggled and warmed at the teasing hunger in his eyes.

'But...' he murmured, stepping towards her so that she could feel the size and girth of his erection. 'I actually wasn't talking about that. I was talking about the house. It has to be big enough for, let's just say, all future additions.'

Ryan couldn't imagine greater contentment. He cupped her head with his hand and kissed her tenderly on her lips. 'And,' he said, moving to hold her tighter and deepening his kiss, 'the sooner we get started on those additions, the better....'

* * * * *

CLASSIC

Quintessential, modern love stories
that are romance at its finest.

EXTRA

REQUEST YOUR FREE BOOKS!

2 FREE NOVELS PLUS 2 FREE GIFTS!

Harlequin *Presents*®

USA TODAY bestselling author

Penny Jordan

brings you her newest romance

PASSION
AND THE PRINCE

Prince Marco di Lucchesi can't hide his proud
disdain for fiery English rose Lily Wrightington—
or his attraction to her! While touring the palazzos
of northern Italy, the atmosphere heats up…until
shadows from Lily's past come out….

*Can Marco keep his passion under wraps
enough to protect her, or will it unleash itself, too?*

Find out in January 2012!

*Brittany Grayson survived a horrible ordeal at the hands
of a serial killer known as The Professional…
who's after her now?*

*Harlequin® Romantic Suspense presents a new installment
in Carla Cassidy's reader-favorite miniseries,*
LAWMEN OF BLACK ROCK.

*Enjoy a sneak peek of
TOOL BELT DEFENDER.*

*Available January 2012
from Harlequin® Romantic Suspense.*

"**B**rittany?" His voice was deep and pleasant and made
her realize she'd been staring at him openmouthed through
the screen door.

"Yes, I'm Brittany and you must be…" Her mind suddenly went blank.

"Alex. Alex Crawford, Chad's friend. You called him
about a deck?"

As she unlocked the screen, she realized she wasn't
quite ready yet to allow a stranger inside, especially a male
stranger.

"Yes, I did. It's nice to meet you, Alex. Let's walk around
back and I'll show you what I have in mind," she said. She
frowned as she realized there was no car in her driveway.
"Did you walk here?" she asked.

His eyes were a warm blue that stood out against his
tanned face and was complemented by his slightly shaggy
dark hair. "I live three doors up." He pointed up the street to
the Walker home that had been on the market for a while.

"How long have you lived there?"

"I moved in about six weeks ago," he replied as they

walked around the side of the house.

That explained why she didn't know the Walkers had moved out and Mr. Hard Body had moved in. Six weeks ago she'd still been living at her brother Benjamin's house trying to heal from the trauma she'd lived through.

As they reached the backyard she motioned toward the broken brick patio just outside the back door. "What I'd like is a wooden deck big enough to hold a barbecue pit and an umbrella table and, of course, lots of people."

He nodded and pulled a tape measure from his tool belt. "An outdoor entertainment area," he said.

"Exactly," she replied and watched as he began to walk the site. The last thing Brittany had wanted to think about over the past eight months of her life was men. But looking at Alex Crawford definitely gave her a slight flutter of pure feminine pleasure.

Will Brittany be able to heal in the arms of Alex, her hotter-than-sin handyman…or will a second psychopath silence her forever? Find out in
TOOL BELT DEFENDER
Available January 2012
from Harlequin® Romantic Suspense
wherever books are sold.

SPECIAL EDITION

Life, Love and Family

Karen Templeton

introduces

The FORTUNES *of* TEXAS: Whirlwind Romance

When a tornado destroys Red Rock, Texas, Christina Hastings finds herself trapped in the rubble with telecommunications heir Scott Fortune. He's handsome, smart and everything Christina has learned to guard herself against. As they await rescue, an unlikely attraction forms between the two and Scott soon finds himself wanting to know about this mysterious beauty. But can he catch Christina before she runs away from her true feelings?

FORTUNE'S CINDERELLA

Available December 27th wherever books are sold!